I0682896

GOLD MAN REVIEW

ISSUE 13

Gold Man Review is published annually by Gold Man Publishing.

The editors invite submissions of previously unpublished works of fiction, nonfiction, and poetry. Manuscripts can be submitted at www.goldmanpublishing.com by following our submission guidelines.

Address all requests to:
Heather Cuthbertson
Editor-in-Chief
Heather.Cuthbertson@GoldManPublishing.com

Contents

FICTION

POETRY

NONFICTION

Issue 13 Editor's Letter

Lucky Number 13.

Or unlucky depending on how superstitious you are. I had to do a little research on superstitions because, well, 13, and apparently billions of people believe in them. There are the common ones: a black cat crossing your path, walking under a ladder, breaking a mirror—seven years bad luck for that one. Come to find out, the superstition of breaking mirrors dates back all the way into Ancient Rome and Greece. Wild.

Just like the broken mirror superstition, the number 13 has its own historical baggage and even comes with a fancy word: triskaidetaphobia. (Now say that five times fast.) The reason why it's not a favorite in the digital sphere is hard to know for sure, but it's believed it originated in 1750 BC to the Code of Hammurabi and the 13th law skipped from the text. Except it wasn't skipped, not intentionally anyway. The code was never listed numerically and what they know is that whoever was translating them missed the line by accident. Nothing but a clerical error, a case of maybe staying up too late the night before or sore eyes, but a blunder that has spiraled through time and speculation.

But that's just one theory.

Some think the reason 13 has such a negative vibe is because it follows the number 12. Somewhere it was decided that 12 was a good and proper number representing completeness and perfection, such as the pureness of the months of the year, signs of the zodiac, the hours on a clockface, the Twelve Days of Christmas, among other great combinations from adding 6+6. But then there comes 13, showing up by sheer virtue of being the next digit in the numerical sequence, and throwing an extra sock on the laundry pile, because, you know, bad.

Another is that 13 got its notoriety because of some famous guests who coincidentally were the 13th to arrive and opted for trouble. There's Judas, the 13th guest at the Last Supper, and Loki, the 13th guest to show at a dinner party where he orchestrated *deicide*. Note to self: Only invite 12 people when throwing any kind of a get-together. Otherwise, someone's about to die.

And what about the notorious Friday, the 13th? That day has its own set of issues.

Airlines don't have a 13th row. Hotels skip 13th floors, so do hospitals. And they won't have a Room 13 either. But just because administrators and CEOs decide not to label a row, a floor, a room, does it really not exist? Should I jump for joy when I breeze past row 12 on my plane and sit in the next labeled 14A? The fact of the matter is whether the number 13 is really such a sinister actor isn't grounded in any kind of observable truth—like cyanide can kill you—but perception. Kind of like, well, everything.

So here we are, lucky or unlucky Issue 13, with contributors throwing their wrenches into the mix of superstition. As always, there's something for everyone, and what I believe, to be a very lucky, a very the-stars-have-aligned blend of fiction, nonfiction, and poetry that falls in step with our style and what we want to offer to readers.

I hope you enjoy what is to come in the following pages and may your life be full of happy coincidences, happenstances, and strokes of luck.

Sincerely,

Heather Cuthbertson
Editor-in-Chief
Gold Man Review

Gold Man Review Editors
Issue 13

Heather Cuthbertson
Editor-in-Chief

Nicklas Roetto
Project Editor

Eric Halpenny
Editor

Kaitlynn Price
Editor

Ashley Rich
Editor

2023 Gold Man Review Readers
Daniel Link
Michaela Elliot

gold man review

FICTION

Jessica Cousin

juliet waller

M y cell phone is ringing, and I'm not answering. I'm sitting on my bed watching as the phone lights up with the words: Jessica Cousin. My cousin never calls. If she does, it means someone has died, and who wants a call like that? Not me, no thank you. I watch the phone, Jessica Cousin on the screen, yelling at me. I know like four Jessicas. Doesn't everyone? Jessica Cousin is one of them. Jessica Grocery Store is another. I listed one of them as Jessica Cunt but autocorrect is a prude, so she is Jessica Count. Fucking Jessica Count. She never calls.

I'm waiting one hundred and fifty dog years for it to stop ringing and go to voicemail. This is endless and then FINALLY, it stops. Then it takes forever for it to register as a message. I probably have osteoporosis by now. Jessica Cousin must be leaving a detailed account of this death. Ok, it's ready. I put Jessica Cousin's voicemail on speaker. She is usually kind of a breathy speaker with an annoying laugh. The laugh itself isn't annoying, it's that it happens after every fifth word. I should have more compassion for nervous laughers, but I don't. I have more compassion for people who cannot make eye contact. Wait, that's not compassion, that's connection. Those are my people. I am those people, too. I look at people's mouths when they talk. Maybe that's why the five words/laugh/five words/laugh people annoy me. I'm getting off topic because Jessica Cousin's voice is not breathy, nor is she laughing. She is crying. She is also yelling at me to look at the paper. The paper? What? I listen again. The newspaper. Is there just one newspaper now? In the world? I listen again. The news. The news. Look at the news. Go to CNN. I use my phone. I find the CNN website. Here is what I read:

Bellingham, WA

Mystery Solved. Two Years Later, Woman Returns to the Place of Her Disappearance.

A whale found beached at Mud Bay in Bellingham, Washington, held the surprise of a lifetime. Nearby residents, who gathered at first light this morning to view the mammal, heard what sounded like knocking from inside. Authorities and marine biologists were called in. Upon opening up the whale, they discovered Tasha Petit, the woman who disappeared under mysterious circumstances two years ago. (Link to: Daughter Claims She Saw Mother Swallowed by a Whale). Ms. Petit has been taken to a local hospital for further evaluation. This is a developing story.

Every cliché about blood freezing and hearts dropping and cold sweat dripping happens to me simultaneously. I reread the article. I don't click on the link. I don't need to because I know I'm the one who's had the word "claims" floating around my head like some fucked up Pig-Pen character for two years. You know what else floats around when you are a twenty-three-year-old human grown-up, and your mother mysteriously disappears, and you are someone who does not make eye contact? The word suspect. The word suspect and the word claims swirl in a constant dust storm around my head. What the fuck is going on, Jessica. Fucking. Cousin?

I get dressed to go out but due to the frozen blood, dropped heart, cold sweat problem, I forget how outfits work, so I put on striped leggings and a polka-dot dress and mismatched socks, a t-shirt, one leg warmer, and a knit hat. I look like a jumble sale. I feel like a jumble sale. I tumble with my jumble out the door and into my car. Then I go back inside and grab my purse. I put four individual-sized packets of goldfish crackers and my cell phone into it. Then I fumble back into my car to drive up to Bellingham to find my long-lost mother.

There are two TV vans with antennas parked outside the hospital. I bet the inside of those vans smell terrible. Like Frito breath and electricity. I might be recognized as a former person of interest—though now I'm just a slightly interesting person—so I put my head down and hold my left arm against my body with my right arm. I walk in hunched over but straighten up as soon as I get through the ER doors. I go right over to the grumpy-looking man behind the "Visitor/Patient Info" desk. I love grumpy people behind desks. I like the challenge of using my personal grump to un-grump them. It's homeopathic.

His name tag reads M. Shannon. Is he French? Is he Monsieur Shannon? M. Shannon looks at me and pushes out his lips and raises his eyebrows. I speak this language. With his face, he is saying, "Yes?"

"My name is Beatrice Petit," I say. And then he keeps his lips out and his eyebrows up but uses his eyeballs to scan me up-and-down. It's really hard to do and I am impressed. I can tell he knows the name, knows who I am, who my mother is. I nod to show him I, too, know who my mother is.

"May I see some ID," he asks but with a period at the end, not a question mark.

I reach into my purse and pull out my driver's license. It's a terrible picture. My old one expired just after they accused me of killing my mother. If you have not experienced that kind of accusation yet, it really fucks with you. I go over that day a lot, usually when I'm practicing insomnia, which I've become very good at by the way, and I am like seventy-five percent sure I didn't kill her, but when police are like, "Well, ma'am, I think you did," you're like, "Oh, shit. Did I? I mean, I've never wanted to kill my mom, but things can happen, I suppose." Being accused of something you're pretty sure you didn't do is stressful in a way that is chunky and does not feel good under your skin. It is pokey and unpleasant. Anyway, I had my new driver's license picture taken while all this was going on and my face looks like someone who is having constant but teeny-tiny electric shocks and isn't sure why and also isn't sure if it's going to get better or get worse.

M. Shannon looks at my ID. He types something into the computer. I adjust my weird clothes. He hands me back my license and says, "Go through those double doors, follow the orange arrows on the floor until you get to the elevators. She is on floor four, room two hundred and two."

I say, "Merci, Monsieur!" and walk away, proud because my accent sounded pretty good.

My mother is slimy. And she stinks. This is because she is covered in whale blubber. I wonder why they haven't given her a sanitizing scrub down yet. I stop a few feet from her bed and say, "You look like you just swam the English Channel."

My mother laughs and says, "Fuck you. I did swim the English Channel." She gestures to my clothes. "Why do you look like a clown on drugs?"

"I got surprised and forgot how to dress," I say.

She does a little jazz hand and says, "Surprise! It's me. How did you find out?"

"Cousin Jessica called me screaming. So, how are you?"

She lifts one of her arms that's attached to an IV and gestures down her body. "They won't let me bathe because they have to do some scientific studies on my slime. I'm donating my body odor to science."

I'm suddenly so overwhelmed at seeing my mother I feel carbonated inside. I don't want this to freak her out, so I try to look real casual, like I'm a denim jacket. I put my hand on my hip and try to think of a nonchalant thing to say, just as the room fills up with people in different colored scrubs. It gets loud and I'm not sure where I'm supposed to stand and what I'm supposed to do with my face, so I pretend I need to pee. The bathroom has all the extra things hospital bathrooms have, like rails and cords to pull if you fall off the toilet and a prison mirror that makes you look guilty and tiny rectangular tiles on the floor. I realize I'm hungry, and the bathroom looks clean enough, so I lean up against the wall and eat a packet of goldfish crackers from my purse. I hear the buzz of people and the beeps of machines through the bathroom door. I hear my mother laugh over the din. Her laugh is loud, from the diaphragm, heavy. If her laugh had a color, it would be dark blue. Comforting blue. It's confirmed I didn't kill my mother, but I still have the chunky feeling under my skin.

There is a knock at the door and a voice says, "You ok in there?"

I go out. There is only one extra person in the room now, a woman in a lab coat, standing next to my mother's bed. My mother says, "Doctor, this is my daughter, Beatrice."

The doctor is young and has an efficient hairdo: a bob with bangs. She is wearing very doctor clothes: sensible gray slacks, a light blue blouse tucked in, a name tag on her lab coat that says "Dr. Chin," and a stethoscope around her neck. Her shoes are ballet flats in gray. I think she might be wearing knee high pantyhose. "Nice to meet you, Beatrice. I'm Doctor Chin. Your mother is doing remarkably well." Dr. Chin's teeth are nice, straight, and white, with little calcium spots. Her upper lip is a tiny bit thinner than her bottom one.

I say, "Thank you" to her nice mouth. I'm not sure why I say thank you. I should probably ask, like, "How much longer does my mother have to live?" but I don't.

Dr. Chin says, "You'll probably be able to take her home by the end of day tomorrow." Then she nods at me, tells my mom that she'll be back later to check in, and leaves.

Dr. Chin does not lie. I take my mother home the next day. She is currently lying on the living room floor with her eyes closed. She tried to get to the upstairs bathroom, but her body is not convinced she's on land. She said it's like walking while being on the teacup ride, which when I think about it, makes me feel pretty spinny as well. I look at her lying there from my seat on the couch and hear the gulp in my brain. The gulp in my brain started happening after her doctor said my mom could come home. The gulp is loud inside my head and sounds like it comes from a cartoon man with a potbelly and a giant, bobbing Adam's apple. It's the gulp of disbelief. Right after I first heard the gulp of disbelief, I started to feel less chunky under my skin.

When she can make it up to the bathroom, my mother takes a shower, then a bath, then another shower. I go to the store to get the things on her very short grocery list:

Extra soft toothbrush
Children's toothpaste
Hair clippers
Chocolate pudding
Rice pudding
Tapioca pudding

After bathing, she spends a lot of time brushing her teeth and then I start to shave her head because whatever is currently growing out of her skull does not resemble hair anymore. Whatever it is, it doesn't have a comparable analogy. Comparable analogy is a term I stole from Cousin Jessica. She said it to me in the early days of my mother being gone and me becoming a suspect. She came over and found me on the floor of the kitchen. I was literally in a puddle of tears. If I think about it now, I might have also wet my pants. Cousin Jessica knelt down right next to me, getting her knees wet. First, she grabbed my shoulders and shook me, not hard, more like she was gently mixing something inside of me. Then she said, "There is no comparable analogy [nervous laugh] to your situation. You will have to figure out how to [nervous laugh] move forward on an unknown path." Then she got me off the kitchen floor and set me up with a routine, a sticker chart, and stickers. Cousin Jessica is very practical even though she is sometimes hysterical and has that unfortunate laugh.

I think moving forward on an unknown path applies now, too. I don't tell my mother about any of this, I just focus on shaving the no-comparable-analogy on her head. I have to use actual force sometimes. I feel like I'm shearing a sheep. I say to her, "Do you think a sheep ever sees someone in a sweater that used to be the wool on their actual sheep body and goes, "Hey, that looks familiar?"

My mother says, "If you make a sweater out of my hair, I'll kill you." I wasn't thinking that because this "hair" is really disgusting and should go into the garbage as soon as possible. I don't tell her that though. Nobody likes to be told their hair is not fit for a sweater. I just say, "Ookay," in a sarcastic way.

"For real, Bea. If you knit a sweater out of my hair, it will end up in a Smithsonian Museum. Probably right next to that guy's longest fingernails, the curly ones. I am not prepared for any part of me to become part of a museum exhibit."

I stop shaving her head and say, "Wait, those fingernails are in a Smithsonian Museum?"

She scoffs and reaches up to feel her bald spots. "Probably. Or Ripley's Believe It or Not!"

"That would be cool," I say and touch her shoulder, so she'll swivel on the closed seat of the toilet. We're in the downstairs bathroom. There's only room for me to stand on one side of her so she has to rotate around when I need to get to another side of her head. Ripley's Believe It or Not makes me think of the Guinness Book of World Records, which makes me wonder if my mom qualifies as a world record holder. I never Googled it, but I bet her stay inside the whale was longer than most people's. I don't ask her what she thinks about it because that might make her want to kill me too. We haven't talked much about her "time away." We will at some point, but she told me she's not ready yet. She just wants to get back to feeling like a human. I understand this predicament. I might feel shitty, but I always felt human.

Over the drone of the buzzer, I ask if she wants to go eat pudding when I've finished with her head. She gives me a thumbs up. I'm starting to feel a little tired. It's night so no big deal, right? But this tired is different. For the past two years, I've been feeling tired but with the chunky feeling under my skin. This is not a good combination for sleeping. But this night, right now, the chunky feeling is dissipating, and the long-lost feeling of relief is settling in. Relief is a very nice feeling and is something like drinking room temperature water from a glass bottle. I start to think I might sleep well tonight. I think about the fact I'll go to sleep and in the morning my mom will be here in this house. She'll be bald and smelly, and her teeth will be a mess, but she'll be my mom, in the morning, here in this house.

Ghosts, Talking

linda ferguson

A string of pearls, an emerald ring, silver candlesticks. My sister, Lisa, says it's not really stealing. I agree we need the money—we can't disappear for free—but I try to tell her we shouldn't take anything from the Swaffords because the girl, Natalie, seems nice to me.

Lisa says, "So you want to be in the army, Henry?"

"It's not that easy."

"Neither is dysentery or reveille."

By this she means I'm already 17, and ever since I can remember, the Major has celebrated my birthday by saying I'll join the service the day I turn 18.

Of course, when I sign up, the Major will be standing right next to me. If only I could use some kind of code so the recruitment officer would know the truth—two fast blinks followed by a single wink could mean, *I'm here against my will, coerced by a crazy man whose idea of "family time" is to stage surprise inspections of our rooms.* "Not rooms—cells," Lisa always insists. In a four-story house with two parlors and plush drapes, she and I have each been allotted a narrow space (in times past, a servant's room, now divided into two) with a bare floor, a small chest of drawers, and a hard bed.

She says if only our mother was here, she'd keep the Major in check: "She made faces behind his back during the morning flag salute, then winked at me."

"She sounds nice," I once said to Lisa.

"Not exactly. She was a smart lady who knew when to leave."

Of course, that's our problem: Lisa and I can't leave. We don't even have the cash for a single bus ticket because the Major has forbidden us to work for anyone but him. He also wouldn't let Lisa take a college class after she graduated from high school last spring. Instead, he informed her she'd be grocery shopping and paying the bills in addition to doing the cooking and cleaning we both always do.

When I look at our situation in this light, stealing from the Swaffords doesn't seem so crazy.

"Check their dining room first," Lisa says, slipping into my room at night when the Major is in his study. (Who knows what the Major studies? How to bend children to your will? How to hold them over a fire until their bones melt?) "Look for sterling. Anything small enough to slip in your backpack. If there's a locked cupboard, you'll need to find a key."

I picture my sister in uniform, an Allied officer planning an attack on a German stronghold. I want to say, "Why don't we just *ask* Natalie Swafford if we can borrow the bus fare?" There are probably even teachers (the ones who've had contact with the Major) who'd give us money. But Lisa gets such a kick out of her schemes. Maybe she doesn't take them all that seriously. Maybe she's just letting her imagination run, and believe me, it needs the exercise. Sometimes we'll be in the same room, reading, and I'll sense her brain buzzing like a yellowjacket around a fallen apple.

That's why I keep quiet when Lisa says Natalie had a great-great-great-aunt who was married to an Austrian Duke and the Swaffords inherited the Duchess's gold-rimmed china that would sell for a thousand dollars apiece. Or when Lisa says they have a collection of Charles Dickens first editions, I don't throw cold water in her face by saying there's no way I can make off with the contents of a library without somebody noticing, and I never ask, "Where did you hear these stories about the Swaffords, anyway? The only person you ever talk to is me."

The last time Natalie and I were in the same class was in eighth grade Spanish. We wrote and performed a skit where her character carried a magic umbrella, *el paraguas*. *"Si, es mi paraguas!"* she announced, twirling a yellow striped umbrella. She was as lumpy as a bowl of oatmeal in the big sweaters she favored. When she laughed, though, she sounded like morning—if your morning didn't include the psychotic shriek of a bugle at 5 a.m., and a father attired in full uniform, all medals, buckles, and snaps.

When we were little, Lisa made a spaceship for me out of a cardboard box and flashlights. I sat inside it and thought I could fly off. Instead, the Major threw open my door, saw me holding two of his flashlights, and marched me down to his study to "have a word with me."

Another time Lisa decided we should start smuggling food.

"As soon as we have enough provisions to last a month, we'll run away," she said with an authority that sounded eerily like the Major.

I slipped crackers into my pockets and stored them in a shoe box under my bed. Lisa kept the food she was saving in her underwear drawer. Our smuggling days ended abruptly without the Major's intervention. One morning, I heard a shriek coming from Lisa's room. When I ran to her, she cried, "I put my hand in the drawer and found a mouse! It was like a plum," she shuddered, "a warm plum that *squirmed*."

I came up with my own escape plan in fifth grade when Kenny, a classmate, complained about his "strict" father. I told him about the Major's surprise inspections and the resulting "disciplinary proceedings." Kenny couldn't believe it.

"You should run away," he said.

"Oh, we will," I replied. "My sister has lots of good ideas."

When I asked the Major permission to go to Kenny's house after school to practice soccer, he scowled in a way that made my bones flinch, then barked that maybe it would toughen me up. The next day I was in Kenny's kitchen, wolfing chocolate chip cookies from a bag. His dad came in and sat with us and asked if he could have a cookie too.

"So, what's your dad really like?" I asked my friend the next day.

"What do you mean?"

"When no one's around. He can't always be that nice."

"For your information," Kenny huffed, "not everybody's parents are lunatics."

Lunatic. The word ran through my head the whole way home. The Major was nuts. Maybe everyone knew this. I started running because I couldn't wait to tell Lisa the good news. If the Major was crazy, it wasn't our fault he was so mean.

"Do you think your parents might adopt me and Lisa?" I asked Kenny one day. "We're pretty quiet and we don't need much to eat."

Kenny liked the idea. He had his mother call the Major to invite Lisa and me over, and the Major was oddly receptive. Lisa, who was listening outside his office, said she heard him laughing with Kenny's mom, but I didn't completely believe her.

The next day at Kenny's house, we drew blue diagrams of his room, planning how we'd fit three beds in it. Kenny said he and I could have bunk beds. Lisa said she'd always wanted a fainting couch and maybe she could have a narrow one by the window, where she could pass the afternoons reading.

That night at dinner, the Major sent Lisa to her room because her fingers were stained with blue ink (a Class 5 infraction). When she almost skipped upstairs, I knew just how she felt. Soon we'd be part of a real family.

I went home with Kenny again the next week.

He was in the bathroom when his mother stopped by the door of his room and said, "You know, Kenny would love to have a brother and sister." I felt my hand squeezing into a fist, somehow sensing what was coming. "But it wouldn't be fair to your father to take you away from him."

She tilted her head, concerned. "Is everything alright at home?" she asked.

"Sure," I said, then surprised myself by adding, "my sister's getting a pony."

I didn't go back to Kenny's house again.

That was the last time Lisa and I made getaway plans. Until this fall when she starts talking about the plot to steal from Natalie's family. Following me upstairs after school one day, she flops on my bed and asks, "Have you talked to her yet?"

"I haven't had class with Natalie in four years. She probably doesn't even remember me."

My sister smiles like she's watching a toddler let off steam. "Henry, have you been in front of a mirror lately? Have you seen how girls look at you?" She pats my cheek. "I'm your big sister, and even *I've* noticed. You're *handsome*, honey."

"Natalie's not like that," I say, taking my binder out of my backpack. Fifteen hundred hours. According to Major Time, I should have been doing homework for the last ten minutes. Lisa and I don't even need clocks to know what we're required to do each moment. Rise and shine, cold shower, push-ups, chores (you really could eat off our parquet foyer floor).

I open my binder. "She's a serious person. She's not going to start batting her eyelashes at me."

"We'll see," says Lisa, winding a lock of her hair tight around her finger. "Do something that makes her take notice."

I shake my head, but Lisa isn't looking at me.

"I've got it," she says, releasing her hair so it springs free. "The school's doing the spelling bee again this year, right?"

"But that's in less than two weeks."

"Which means we've got to work fast."

"But—"

Lisa stands up and salutes. "Hup, two, three, four," she chants and marches around my room.

I agree to sign up for the spelling bee.

Lisa makes me practice every night. I pace the room while she sits cross-legged on my narrow bed and reads words aloud like they're dessert. When she says *algorithm*, I picture a piece of cream-filled pastry in her mouth. With *deciduous*, it's more like she's licking a popsicle with the tip of her tongue. Every evening we cover more of the list. *Eucalyptus, fortissimo, ophthalmologist.*

We study for more than two hours the night before the big event. My voice is raspy on *baccalaureate* and becomes a rusty hinge when I get to *porraceous*.

"Not bad," Lisa says. "Let's just run through the list one last time." It's 10:15, and if the Major discovers we're breaking curfew—no *fraternizing* (spelling word) after 2200 hours – someone may be composing a *requiem* for us. I drop beside her on the bed and close my eyes. "On second thought," she says, "we're probably good." I don't hear her leave.

In the morning my throat feels like I've swallowed a broken seashell.

"Good news," Lisa says as I take my seat at the table. "The Major's 'meeting' ran extra late last night, so it's just you and me for breakfast." She sets down a small white bowl of strawberries beside my oatmeal.

I pick up my spoon and set it down again.

"Lisa," I whisper, even though we're alone, "I think I've got a fever."

"Nerves, silly," she says. "Have some tea."

Maybe she's right because I feel better once I'm at school. The words are my friends, and we're dancing. In the end it's just Natalie and me. The pronouncer, an English teacher, keeps tossing balls (*supercilious, ziggurat, efflorescence*), and we keep catching them until she announces we have a tie. I shake Natalie's hand, but when I turn to leave the stage, my knees buckle. The school nurse calls home, and the Major, who Lisa later tells me was still in bed, says I can make my way home on the bus.

"Our plan is working," Lisa says when she slips into my room that evening. "Natalie called to ask how you're doing. I told the Major it was your counselor."

I have a fever and have to stay home for a week. When I finally go back to school, I stop by my locker and there is Natalie, who seems to be waiting for me.

"Oh hi," she says, a little breathlessly. She has a new haircut and is touching the ends. "So, you have Mr. Ramirez for history, don't you?" she asks. "I have him fifth period, and I was wondering if you'd want to borrow my notes." She touches her hair again. "I made copies."

In English that afternoon, we're watching a video of *Othello*. As the moor of Venice presses a pillow against his wife's face, I write in a corner of my notebook, *Flowers for Natalie?* But there are no flowers in our yard, just a sharp-edged lawn and the boxwood hedge the Major insists I trim with surgical precision. I begin sketching an idea for a card—a magic *paraguas*. I finish the card that night and slip it into her locker on Friday.

On Monday she stops me in the hall. "I liked your card. So did my mom."

She showed my card to her mom?

"Well, I should let you get to class," she finally says. Again, she lifts her hand to her hair and starts to walk away.

"Natalie?" I call. *This is for Lisa*, I tell myself. "Would you have time to go over your notes with me?"

Natalie isn't Kenny, I remind myself as we leave school together. Her house is dirty white with a wide porch and a jungle of lavender so overgrown it's falling over. I follow her through the door and into the living room. The first thing I see is a giant painting of three women over the fireplace, arms entwined.

"My aunt took an art class last summer," Nathalie explains.

There's nothing else to see. No sumptuous rugs inherited from silken ancestors. No tasseled pillows or wall tapestries or antique Japanese figurines. Certainly no Charles Dickens first editions. Just a pale green couch fading to beige, an armchair, and a bookcase lined with paperbacks. Where *did* Lisa get the idea the Swaffords were rich?

There's a sound at the door. A woman comes in carrying a laptop and a bulging bag of groceries.

"So," Natalie's mother says, smiling, "this is Henry."

That evening Lisa pounces. Clutching my arm, she tells me to draw every room I saw.

"Can't that wait?" I ask, wanting to hold onto the pictures in my mind: Natalie, waving a tortilla chip as she talked. Lemon colored kitchen walls and three buttery roses, fully opened, floating in a bowl of water. Ms. Swafford, a widow, setting her groceries on the couch so she can shake my hand (*Call me Pattie*, she said).

"No, Henry, it can't wait." My sister pulls me up the stairs to her room.

"Lisa, the Swaffords aren't as loaded as we thought."

"Maybe they keep the really valuable things on the second floor. Sit," she says, then leans over me with crackling eagerness and hands me a black pen.

"They have an entry hall, right? Start with that. I'm serious. We've got to do it like this."

I draw an entry hall, even though the house doesn't have one. I put a tall coatrack in the corner, heaped with raincoats. In the opposite corner, I add an umbrella stand. I imagine it as a pale blue porcelain with blush-pink birds spiraling around it.

"Yes, this is exactly what we need," Lisa says, gripping my shoulder.

I go home with Natalie again.

"Have you used their bathroom, Henry?" Lisa asks later, after the Major has left for another "meeting."

"Is this something I should be telling you?"

"If you've seen their bathroom you've got to draw it," she says, with a rap on my sketch pad.

With colored pencils this time, I add a border of swans to peach towels. Purple blooms on an African violet on the windowsill. Then I draw myself in front of the toilet, producing a pale, golden arc.

"Henry, what do you think we're doing here?" Lisa, who's leaning over my shoulder, demands.

I muss her hair, the same dark brown as mine. *Near-twins*, she used to call us. *Better than the ordinary kind.*

"School's out," I say as I jump up and run down the stairs, knowing she'll chase me. Even in a skirt and heels (the Major requires us to dress for dinner), I can feel her pounding feet right behind me.

The Major has started to attend more and more "meetings." When he comes home a strange smell rolls up the stairs. For some reason I imagine a pot of crème de menthe scalding on a stove. I always want to relish his absences, but Lisa insists we work on "The Plan" whenever he's out. One evening she says we'll begin our "preparatory exercises." Lying on her bed with her eyes closed, she tells me to creep about her room as quietly as possible and take something. "I'll count to thirty," she says, "and then I'll open my eyes and try to find what's missing."

"Lisa," I laugh, "it's not like I'm going to sneak around Natalie's house while she and her mom are *sleeping*!"

"Get serious, Henry," she says in the brisk tone she uses whenever I drag my feet. "We need to be ready for all eventualities."

"*All eventualities?* Look, if there's any eventuality involving me getting caught and sent to prison, then you can count me out right now!"

"Fine!" Before I know it, she's off the bed and swinging her pillow at my head, which wouldn't hurt except the cover has a metal zipper. "Fine. Fine. Fine!" she says hitting my face again and again until my chin stings.

"Christ, Lisa, I'm bleeding."

"Good!" she hisses and strikes me again.

"Would you listen for one goddamn minute?"

"Infraction! Infraction!" she barks. "That's two. One for raising your voice and one for cursing."

"Shut up!"

"Shh! What's that? Do I hear the sound of a polished shoe on the stair? He's coming for you, Henry. He's coming." It's her kaleidoscope eyes that stop me, wheeling prisms of excitement.

"What's wrong with you? If he kills me, that's going to leave you awfully lonely, sister."

"To hell with you! To hell with you!" she screams and throws herself on the bed, sobbing.

I spring across the room and press her face into the mattress to muffle the sounds of her crying. "Are you out of your mind? What if he does come home? He'll murder us both."

"Good," she sobs, twisting to free herself. "Let him." She raises her wet face. "Let him kill us both and get caught doing it, too!"

I drop beside her on the bed. She twists away from me, leaving her wet hair strewn behind her on the pillow. I'm on my back, staring at the bare lightbulb above us. When I squint the light extends into the shape of dragonfly wings. "If he was convicted," I whisper, as if the Major was just outside her door, "do you think he'd get life or just the death penalty?"

"Life," Lisa says, her voice shaking. In fact, all of her is shaking, and we're so close I feel as if I am too. "In the smallest, coldest, darkest, cell they've got."

"And we'd be free," I say.

"Yes."

"Dead, but free."

"Not dead-dead, though," Lisa says, her voice steadying. "We'd be ghosts."

"Alright, we'd be ghosts. Would we haunt his prison?"

"Maybe. If we felt like it, we'd drift into his cell now and then and laugh like maniacs." She rolls to face me.

"I'd like that," I say. "What would we do with the rest of our time?"

I'm still on my back. When I was younger, I used to imagine lying on a scaffold like Michelangelo and painting pictures on the ceiling for Lisa to see whenever she heard the Major coming for her. Back then she was always asking for pictures of women in ruffled dresses and feathered hats. Now I think she'd like wild animals, like a hyena baring its teeth.

"We'd live here," she says. "Just the two of us. We'd have flowers and candles and music everywhere and we'd slide down the banister and sleep in a different room every night. We'd always leave the windows and doors open—even in winter, so the snow could blow in and make little drifts."

"Can't we have any other company? How about a girl ghost for me?"

"We'll have a bird," she says. "A beautiful bird with black claws and a hooked beak and shining emerald wings, swooping through rooms and landing where it will."

Lisa snuggles closer to me, digging her sharp chin into my shoulder. I'm thinking about a conversation we once had.

I'd asked her, "How are you ever going to meet someone to love with the Major standing guard?"

She'd been scraping her hair back into a ponytail so tight I half-expected to see tears in her eyes. "Why would I want to meet anyone else?" she'd said. "You and I are a pair."

I get off the bed now. "Close your eyes, Lisa."

I look around the bare room. There's literally nothing to steal, but we can both pretend.

Skip a Life

oliver reimers

John came by the convenience store last night. I was counting cash for the day when the bell above the door jostled. It doesn't ring anymore, rather clicks. I've been meaning to replace it for weeks. I busied myself with arranging the bills while whoever entered perused the aisles. Then John set a pack of Camels on the counter, and I had no choice but to ring him up. Of course, he was buying cigarettes. He always bought cigarettes. I stayed quiet—took his cash, gave him change. I didn't meet his eyes. My muscles tightened. He'd make some snide remark soon, or he'd sigh and glare so hard I'd feel it.

But he took his cigarettes and left. I should've stayed to close the store, cleaned the floors caked with Winter mud, but I locked the cash register, turned off the lights, and locked the door. John was a block away by now, just by the crosswalk. I ran to him. Insane, I know. My ears numbed, and my breath patterned the air in front of me. Snow on the forecast, they said. Be prepared for tonight. Once a year, it snows like this. Just a few inches, but it snows.

John glanced back at me, and for the first time in a year, our eyes met. I wore the scarf he gave me years ago. I stumbled to a halt at the crosswalk, and he sidestepped. I pursed my lips to keep from saying anything. Like always, I'd mess things up.

The crossing light changed, and we walked across the street. Still, John didn't look in my direction. We passed by dead shops and light-less houses. Only a diner on the corner dared stay open this late. We reached it, and John pushed the door in. He held it open a second longer for me to squeeze in behind him. The checkered floor almost made me nauseous. The stools at the counter were empty save for two teens, a boy and a girl, sharing a milkshake like they do in the movies. I always wanted to do that but never could. For some reason, it's weird when it's a boy and a boy.

I sat across from John in a booth and waited for the waitress to come. When she did, John ordered a pound cake. She brought it in minutes, and John took a knife and carved the cake in half. He nudged a half towards me. I picked at the cake. It crumbed between my fingers, so I fit it in my mouth before it could mess up the whole table. I'd forgotten how much he liked pound cake. We'd been to this diner a few times before when I was maybe nineteen. Before it all fell apart. We'd take pound cake from wherever we could find it and eat it at the park. After finishing, John would smoke and ramble about things he said I couldn't understand because I was too young. He was twenty years older and had more life experience. He understood things.

After we finished the cake, I followed John across the street. He always scrutinized the streets for any hint of headlights before crossing. Streetlights fanned over us, stark shadows ridging his face. When I was younger, I thought he was handsome. His eyes reminded me of my room when I was little, a soft blue I used to run to when I was scared. His face seemed judging when you didn't know him, but it could be soft, and his cheeks would crease when he smiled in a way that made me forget everything he'd done. Now his smile just made me quiet.

We headed down the sidewalk to the park. Dew sleeked the benches and slides, but John sat anyway, me after. The dampness clinging to my pants didn't help the cold. I slid closer to John until our legs pressed together. It was like when were together, and I could rest my head on his shoulder and drown out everything but the warmth, wait until he finished his rants to go home. Like then, I reverted to a natural state when I was with him: legs tensed in anticipation, hands ready to dart up and cover my neck.

Cold melded onto my nose. Specks of white peppered the ground. Snow here was more slush than anything. It hit the ground white but sloshed together in a frigid mess. John grabbed my arm. My spine jolted, and I instinctively tugged my arm back. He glared at me. I took a breath. He was only trying to lead me away from the bench, back to somewhere safe from the snow.

I stayed a step behind him as we walked through the streets. A shape loomed a street ahead. I knew it was the church. Where else would we go? I resigned myself to the back of my mind, a spectator to what would happen. The sides of my vision fogged. When John opened the church door, I hardly knew I walked in. When he grabbed my hand, I barely felt it. Our footsteps echoed to the reaches of the ceiling. We entered his room. He ran Summer and Winter camps at the church and got a room because of it.

We met at his summer camp when I was seventeen. He hit some of the boys there and yelled at all of us, told us we'd burn in Hell for being rotten homosexuals. But he was always nice to me. I was special, he said. He gave me presents; books and scarves and a room to myself. He'd call me into his room and talk to me until I dozed off. All he wanted was someone to talk to. I was safe with him, he assured me. I believed him.

I met a man at a bar a month back. It was in San Francisco, three hours from my home, but I was desperate for connection. Rent be damned, I drained my pockets on gas money and rode to San Francisco on a limb. I ate crab at Fisherman's Wharf and watched grizzled men haul cages from the ocean. I tried on jean jackets and sweaters at small shops and asked the clerk what he thought. I looked in the changing room mirrors and marveled at the fact I could go without a scarf to hide my bruises.

In the evening, I went to Twin Peaks Tavern in a district I'd heard about. It was a new gay bar, and I was barely old enough to drink, so it would be a good first experience for me. I pored over the menu and ordered a mimosa because the rest of the drinks were too unfamiliar. It stung when I sipped it. I took a table in the back and endured the rest of my mimosa.

That's when I met the man. His face is unclear to me, a haze of half-drunken memories, but cigarettes scented him. He sat beside me and offered me a drink. I was incapable of saying no. I forced down a cocktail and listened to him smooth-talk me: I had a nice face, I looked a little lost and he could help me, asked if I wanted to dance. I agreed to dance. He led me to the thick of the crowd, and I put my hands on his shoulders like the couples did in my high school dances. He laughed and told me it wasn't that kind of dance. My face heated and my brain prickled, but he kissed me, and I clung to him the rest of the night. I laughed when he made bad jokes and grinned my face off when he took me outside to smoke. I found myself craving pound cake.

He took me back to his house, and by then, I was in love with him.

He asked if I wanted anything else to drink, and I said sure and grimaced as I took another shot. Anytime he asked if I wanted something, I said, sure, go ahead, I don't mind. I let him do what he wanted. I think I passed out at three AM.

In the morning, he made me eggs and some drink to help me with my hangover. I finished, and he handed me my keys I'd left on his nightstand and said he'd had a good time. He urged me towards the door.

"I live too far to visit often," I said. I fingered my keys. "I can get an apartment here or something. I like this city—"

"This wasn't supposed to be anything serious," the man said. I wish I could remember his face.

My face flared. "It wasn't?"

"I get it. You don't know how these things work." He tangled his fingers through his hair. "I don't want to make a thing out of this. We had a nice time, and that's all."

The teeth of my keys ground against my palm. "You should've told me."

"I assumed you knew. Now, can you please leave?"

"But I'm in love with you," I blurted.

He opened the door. "No, you're not."

I stumbled out, unable to say no. The lock clicked behind me. Fog misted my eyelashes, my hair, and my head curdled with hangover. I thought of John. I kept thinking of him as I fumbled through the city to find the bar where my car still was. Amidst the sting of fumes and grip of fog, a sort of hollowness filled me. It wasn't new. I'd felt it constantly before John and with John, but it was only after I left him it became apparent. I wanted to be numb. Numb like bare feet in the snow, so detached not even a car rolling over them could be felt. I wanted to spectate my own life, have everything feel as if it were happening to another person, one I barely knew. All vividness and vibrance would bleed away, and I would be so unfeeling, I'd hardly know I was there.

I achieved this last night with John. My life became a photograph I could look at but never enter. I was vaguely aware I didn't want to stay in his room with him, I didn't like the feeling of his skin against mine, but it didn't matter. I waited for it to be over, and at last it was. John bit at the end of a cigarette and beckoned me outside. I followed.

We went to the side of the church and leaned against the wall. This was routine for us when I still lived at the church with him. He lit his cigarette and sucked in, then drew it away. Smoke ringed the air. "I'm quitting conversion therapy, you know," he said. There was a slight rasp to his voice I never noticed until then. "Once the Winter session is over, I'm done."

Slight shock registered with me. "Really?"

"It makes me sad. They'll all grow up broken and end up breaking others." He took a draw on his cigarette. It was natural for him, an extension of breathing.

"Why'd you even do it in the first place if it makes you sad?"

He shrugged. "I thought it'd make up for being a sexual deviant."

I rubbed my hands over my arms. "But you did terrible things there."

A puff of smoke slipped from his lips. "Yeah. Well, sometimes the things people do to get into Heaven are worse than the things that land them in Hell." He took the cigarette from his mouth with two fingers. "We all turn into broken people. Society calls us wrong and turns us into monsters."

And suddenly, I was aware of the rancidness of smoke in my nostrils, the bitter clamp of cold against me, the hollowness I couldn't distance myself from no matter how hard I tried. There was sweat beneath my clothes and a car radio a block down and the rich scent of tomatoes. I was with John. Why was I with John? I was stupid to go after him, stupider than I'd been when I drove to San Francisco and thought things would change. A fly brushed my arm, and I thought I'd vomit if I smelled cigarette smoke any longer. I was hit with such reality I wanted to cry.

"I'm not broken," I said. I knew he'd hit me or go on one of his rants about how I'm so stuck up and think I'm so much better than him. I prepared to flinch.

He held the cigarette close to his mouth. "Yeah?"

I nodded.

He sighed. "Well, maybe you're different." He cast his cigarette aside and headed for the door of the church. I stayed as the last of the cigarette flames smoldered in the snow.

The Mannequin of Lot 18

nicole pyles

At first, the mannequins moved slowly. The ones without faces crept around the store, careful to avoid bumping into shelves. The mannequins with faces and bodies paid close attention to the fleshy presence of customers sorting through racks of clothes. Heads on shelves blinked and stared as people reached around them. The ones without any head at all stayed in place, tapping the top of their neck where their head should have been.

It made everyone uncomfortable, but no one knew how to get rid of them. Stores were confused as to why only the mannequins of their city were moving. They considered replacing them with the still versions available in other parts of the country, but people thought it seemed inhumane to take them out of their familiar roles. A burgeoning group of activists organized protests across the city. They carried signboards demanding the mannequins receive citizenship, a fair living wage with benefits, and protection through labor laws. Many people protested giving them any sort of help at all.

Dell didn't care either way. He just didn't want to bus them around anymore.

"Come on inside. Hurry it up!" he yelled out to a group of 25 mannequins waiting at the bus stop in front of lot 18. The early morning sun glimmered off the stop, signaling the start of his first shift of the day.

The recently established OHM—Organization of Humanized Mannequins—had made progress by insisting the working mannequins receive subsidized housing paid for by the city and the stores employing them. Some resided in a remodeled warehouse located miles away from any real people. On top of that, the city paid bus drivers time-and-a-half to take them to and from their store jobs in the downtown area. With all the bonus pay, Dell needed ten more paychecks to finally afford to put the city behind him.

The mannequins boarded without saying a word. Each one wore an outfit personally chosen by designers who wanted to advertise away from the store. Even the ones that were only heads were matched with the headless bodies and now donned elaborate jewelry, colorful hats, and fancy outfits. There were problems, of course. At least the confused and angry public stopped throwing as much food at the mannequins anymore. Even the number of obscenities yelled at the bus had cut down.

Finally, the female mannequin with soft lavender hair boarded next. She wore a black dress with splashes of purple, complementing her hair. Dell's heart quickened as she chose the seat closest to him. He had seen her on the bus before, but this time she had a realness in her eyes. Like somewhere inside was a real person.

"Sit down, everyone," he said, pulling the doors closed with a lever, ignoring his dizzying thoughts. "There's an accident on I-205. We're behind schedule."

When he checked his mirrors, she caught his gaze. *She's not real,* he reminded himself. Confused, he focused back on the road and maneuvered around the long driveway towards the exit. Twenty-foot-high hedges and sizzling electric fences surrounded the lot holding the mannequins. Although city officials insisted those measures were necessary for security, it reminded Dell of a prison.

He stopped at the security station and showed his pass to the guard. "Great day we're having, huh?"

Ignoring him, the guard grimaced and wordlessly lifted the barrier.

Dell's already lonely life had worsened when he started driving the mannequins around. He had even quit his weekly card game because of a few guys' taunts about his job. Some encouraged Dell to trap the things and set them on fire. The small city showed its ugliness with its intolerance of the strange creatures. Those still-faced beings bore standing in one place for hours while nosey people stared and took pictures. Who would want that job?

Once on the road, Dell tried to make conversation as a force of habit. "So, did you guys catch the game last night?"

None replied.

His real passengers would banter back and forth with him. Some caused trouble, especially the evening crowd, but he appreciated the noise. Ever since his divorce ten years back, he hated the silence at home.

Insisting on filling the void, he carried on with his one-sided conversation. "What's on the agenda today?"

Nothing. No flash of recognition he had said a word. Not even a look of confusion to try and understand his words. They just stared out the window. Except for her. The one with the lavender hair. She listened to him. It was in her eyes.

No, he told himself. One day, they'd return to being the still, silent figures everyone ignored.

"For me," Dell continued. "Once I drop you folks off, I drive around the regular people. The perk about you mannequins is you don't cause trouble. Real people are obnoxious. Messier too."

He repositioned the rearview mirror to catch her attention. If he didn't know any better, she was smirking, about to laugh at his comment.

A mile down on the empty rural highway, a woman stood next to a brand-new sports car and waved at his bus, trying to catch his attention.

Despite his reservations, Dell pressed on the breaks and maneuvered to the side of the road a few yards ahead of her car. People rarely drove along this isolated highway, in part due to the GPS scramblers put in place by the local government. No one was meant to find the mannequins, although a few attempted anyway and drove around in circles. Unless he pulled over for her, she would wait for hours.

From the side mirror, he watched as she made her way over.

"Bet you see this rich type all the time," he remarked. Behind him, the mannequin with the lavender hair smiled at his comment. His chest swelled with pride. He couldn't remember the last time he made someone beautiful laugh, mannequin or otherwise.

As the well-kept woman reached the bus, Dell pulled the lever to open the doors. Without hesitating, she stepped inside, stinking of overpowering perfume, bringing in too much reality so early in the morning.

"Can you give me a lift? My car stalled and—" She gasped in delight and her eyes danced, as she absorbed each immovable face. Then Dell spotted the press badge at her waistband.

He panicked and opened the doors again, resisting the urge to physically push her away. "A reporter, huh? L-listen, lady," he said, fighting the same stutter that popped up during every confrontation he'd had his entire life. "I-I can't help you. I might lose my job over this. I-I'll tell the gas attendant you're out here."

"No, please." Her eyes flashed with fear. "I've been out here for hours. It will be off the record. I swear."

"Fine, take a seat then," Dell said, shrugging. When he glanced back, the mannequin with the lavender hair scowled at him. Rattled, he mouthed an apology to her. "But I-I'm only taking you to the gas station," he blurted to the reporter.

The reporter whooped in victory and stepped behind the yellow line. Dell checked his mirrors and maneuvered back on the road. She gripped the bar nearest to him, swaying back and forth as the bus rumbled along.

Finally, the reporter broke her silence. "How long have you been driving them?"

Dell grimaced and tightened his lips.

The reporter chuckled. "Just asking. Not as a reporter, I promise."

"About six months," he replied, uncertain if his strict non-disclosure agreement included such a simple question.

"I think it's spooky. Like moving dolls. What's your name?"

"Dell."

"Dell," she repeated. She stuck her hand out. "I'm Janice."

Dell gripped the wheel, ignoring her.

"Of course," she said, taking it back. "Hands on the wheel."

Soon, the empty landscape transformed. Stores, homes, apartment buildings, and sidewalk vendors populated either side of the road. When people figured out which road he drove along, some even camped out overnight to catch a glimpse of the phenomenon.

Soon the gas station emerged into view, and Dell turned on his blinker to pull to the side of the road. Cars honked and closed around him until a blessed few let him through, allowing him to stop by the sidewalk. A few people seated outside at a nearby outdoor cafe got out of their seats to see him. Dell opened the doors. "Alright, this is where I leave you, ma'am."

She stepped down carefully, not saying another word. At the last step, she turned and dug something out of her purse.

"Here. If you ever want to share your story," she said, handing him a business card.

Dell accepted it and put it in his front pocket. "Go on now. I have to get back on the road." Some people stopped their cars to take a better look, while a gas station attendant took his phone out and started filming.

Safely on the sidewalk, she waved as the doors closed. Dell pulled away from the gas station, imagining what his boss might say about picking up a real person on this route. A reporter, no less. He reminded himself he did a good deed, and whatever happened, at least he helped someone.

Feeling her still glaring behind him, Dell no longer worried about his boss being mad at him. "I won't call her."

In response to the fuming silence, he switched on the radio. An announcer talked about politics and the upcoming election. Dell grunted in annoyance and turned to a station playing country music. He hummed to Willie Nelson and tapped his fingers on the steering wheel in rhythm to an unfamiliar country singer. As much as he tried to ignore her, her eyes burrowed into the back of his neck.

When he reached downtown, he switched off the radio. As the tall buildings loomed overhead, he thought of how fast new stores had populated and how many people moved to the city over the last several months. Influencers from around the world paid thousands to reserve store time to see the mannequins in person. Some places even required customers to agree to a minimum purchase before being allowed inside. The city was too expensive for people like him.

The first stop was at a major department store. Armed guards stood ready to help the sales staff who guided the mannequins inside. Meanwhile, crowds of people pressed against each other and clutched cell phones to film them.

He stopped and the crowds yelled in excitement. Once the guards gave him the signal, Dell opened the doors. The first batch filed out, and staff escorted the mannequins to safety. Then he pulled the bus back onto the street. Eight blocks later, he hit another department store, and sales staff guided the others away.

Three remained, including her. Dell checked his mirrors again, and this time she stared at him without the anger in her eyes. Instead, her face softened as if she wanted to say something.

He reached the other stop and the other two got off, finally leaving only her. Dell's heart raced. It reminded him of when he first met his ex-wife. How could he have any feelings about someone who wasn't human?

Nonetheless, Dell grabbed the reporter's business card out of his front pocket. He ripped it in half and showed her the pieces in the mirror. "See, I meant it. I won't call her." He pulled over when he arrived at her stop. "I'll see you tomorrow, right?"

Quietly, she stood with a smile on her face.

"Hey," Dell called out as she passed him.

She paused.

"Do you ever get tired of doing it? Modeling for folks?"

She remained quiet as she surveyed the empty seats. Then turned back to him, asking a similar question with her eyes.

"I'm a little tired of my job too," Dell admitted. "Maybe one day, we'll both leave this place. Get out of this rut we're in, huh?"

She gazed at him for a long time, as if she wanted to tell him something. Then changing her mind, she nodded.

Dell froze with desperation. *What did she sound like when she spoke? Did she laugh? Did she dream at night?*

The saleswoman knocked on the closed doors, interrupting his trance. Unnerved, he opened them, and the mannequin with the lavender hair was quickly led away.

Frustrated, and yearning for more, Dell drove to the bus station to start his next shift driving for regular people.

The bus depot was empty during the mid-morning hours, most drivers off in other parts of the city, picking up regular people. Dell parked his bus in the lot specifically designed for the drivers like him, already missing his silent companion with the lavender hair. Taking one more look up and down the bus—sometimes the mannequins occasionally dropped an earring or scarf he would turn into his boss—he then grabbed his backpack and left with the doors closing behind him.

"Hear any talk yet?" A voice destroyed by hard-living cackled near Dell. It was his friend, Buzz. He missed their weekly poker nights from before. Maybe life would go back to normal one day. Or he'd find a way out before he got into deep trouble because of those things.

"Eh?" Buzz prompted, limping on his right knee, where he'd been shot once. He never told anyone what happened but insisted he won the fight.

"So far, not a peep," he said, wracking his brain for a way to change the subject.

"Well, it beats out the real people. A lady from my fare last week came on again and complained about having to move her seat for someone in a wheelchair."

On their way to the bus depot break room, Buzz yammered about several indignant passengers and their many complaints.

Once inside, Dell unrumpled a couple of dollars from his pocket to purchase a wilted turkey club and soda from the vending machines. They settled into small white tables and chairs with uneven legs and started in on their lunch. Buzz brought out a hearty-looking sub sandwich, likely made by his wife. Together for nearly 20 years, he complimented her voraciously, insisting he married over his head. The stories he'd share made Dell miss being married, although lately, he barely needed to look at old photos since driving the mannequins around.

"Hey fellas."

In walked Rufus, Dell's junior by a few years, and far too confident for a bus driver, as if he drove a limo instead of facing the harsh realities of public service.

Buzz mumbled a greeting, shoving a chip into his mouth full of sandwich. Dell waved.

Rufus dragged over one of the wobbly plastic chairs and joined their table, tearing into a bag of cheese puffs. Like Dell, he brought in store-bought food, most likely because he hadn't kept a woman long enough for her to want to make a meal for him to take to work.

"So, Mr. Chauffeur of the Silent, how is it going these days?"

"Not a word!" Buzz piped in, cackling with his mouth agape, breadcrumbs spitting out on the table.

Rufus chuckled. "That's what I thought. You won't hear a word. What would they say? Talk about clothes?"

The two men shared a laugh without Dell. In the back of his mind, he knew the woman with the lavender hair had plenty to say. Her eyes looked smart.

"Well, it's better than my other routes," Dell said as if to remind Buzz of his earlier complaints. "Plus, I'm finally saving money."

"You're saving 'cause you quit playing poker! You practically gave us your money!" Buzz guffawed and quickly became serious again. "You fixing on leaving here still?"

"Sure am. Can't do this much longer. The people, you know?"

His two lunch companions agreed and continued discussing the irate passengers each encountered. Dell hoped neither one pressed for the whereabouts of the lot. He needed to protect her.

"Can you believe it? They gave them housing! And job protection!" Rufus pointed out, bringing the conversation back to the mannequins.

Buzz smacked the table. "They aren't even people!"

Rufus leaned forward, dropping his voice to a whisper. "Did you see the post online? About what's going on tonight?" When Dell and Buzz shook their head no, his eyes lit up, eager to share the news. "Some of us are going out there."

"Where?" Dell asked, hoping it was a protest, instead of what he feared the most.

"The lot where those things live. A buddy of mine shared a post on Facebook." Rufus must've noticed the stunned look on Dell's face. "Don't look so surprised. I know you needed to keep your job, so I didn't bother you to tell me where they're at."

"There's no reason to b-bug them, Rufus." Dell said. "W-would you want to stand all day? Have p-people staring at you? Like you're a st-statue?"

The men balked at him, neither moving a muscle.

"My man," Rufus said. "You've been driving them too long. Did one get to you?"

Buzz coughed to clear his throat. "Come on pal, you've been weird about those things. Why don't you come over for poker? Forget all about them and the talk about leaving too."

Dell gazed at the table, refusing to meet their gaze. An old argument with his wife bubbled to the surface. *You're so afraid of everything*, she once said. "No one got to me. There's more than what you see, y-you know."

Silence hovered in the air until Rufus broke it. "There you go. We have to get our city back. You're changing too, man, and not for the better."

Nervous, Dell grabbed his backpack and tossed his lunch away. "Time to start my route."

As Dell turned to leave, Rufus called out for him. "And don't say nothing!"

"Yeah, we know where you live!" Buzz cackled.

The comment stung as Dell left his two friends behind to discuss their plans. He knew one thing. He had to do something.

For six hours, while driving around noisy real-life people, Dell considered every possible way out, then finally concluded.

His first stop of the night would be his last.

At her corner, she stared straight ahead, waiting for the doors to open. He pulled the lever and she quietly stepped inside, choosing the seats nearest to him. He searched her face for signs of life, needing her to speak. Her eyes met his, and uncertainty tugged at the corner of his mind.

Dell pulled onto the road, focusing on the words he had practiced all day, unwilling to change his mind. "Let's get out of here."

Her eyes met his in the rearview mirror.

"Listen, there's something happening tonight. Someone's coming after you guys, and I refuse to let anything happen to you." Dell rambled. "Anyway, if I don't leave now, I never will. I want you to come with me."

She hesitated as if calculating her options or wondering if he was hiding ulterior motives.

The pause made him sweat. Until she nodded. Relieved and excited, Dell pulled over. The sales staff at the stop ahead wouldn't suspect anything for at least 20 minutes.

Dell extended his hand out to her, and she took it, her hand noticeably cool from the air-conditioned store. With his other hand, he checked his pocket, feeling the scraps of paper inside the fabric. His final step included a curious reporter who loved a good story.

They stepped outside with a spattering of people walking around the empty city streets. Dell took the rare moment as a sign and pointed in the direction where he parked his car. Jogging past an office building, the sun reflected golden against the windows, and hope rose in his chest for the first time in years. Then she tugged his hand.

Her face appeared different. A little color brightened her cheeks and a streak of black colored her hair. Her hand even felt warm.

"What's happened to you?" he asked.

"I-I-I-don't know," she muttered through partially opened lips. "I think it's a good thing."

Her voice. He wanted her to say something else. To tell him what she thought about all those days together on the bus. He wanted so much more.

"Me too," Dell managed to say.

"What about the others?" she asked, her eyes searching his.

"I have a plan, but we need to get to my car, okay?" Reaching the parking lot, they got inside his beaten-up old Chevy. He dug the torn business card from his pocket and brought out his cell phone tucked between the front seats. He dialed the number, hoping she answered.

"This is Janice," said the voice on the other line.

"Janice, this is Dell. I have a story for you, but you have to hurry."

That night, news broke of a mob finding the mannequins of lot 18. They were thwarted by the local police waiting on the other side of the gates. Janice Thompson, a local reporter, arrived at the scene with the authorities. She convinced the police of the plot by sharing several Facebook posts of locals encouraging each other to show up with pickaxes and flamethrowers.

No one harmed a single mannequin. Once the officers arrested the men, and the news died down, store owners began to send the mannequins to different locations around the globe. It was far too stressful to keep them around.

Strangely, no one found the one with the lavender hair. Officials assumed she wandered away amid the chaos, and with all the mess it caused in the city, they were relieved. It was one less mannequin to worry about.

As for Dell, no one knew what happened to him either. Later, his boss had gotten a call from him, saying he quit. Soon after, his departure became a tall tale people shared in passing.

If people had searched harder for Dell, they might have found him hundreds of miles away, driving in his Chevy with someone who looked like the mannequin with the lavender hair. Yet, it wasn't a mannequin at all. Not anymore.

Jimmy's Place

tim haywood

"How do we feel about the new shirt?" Jimmy asked himself as he studied his fresh purchase in the bathroom mirror. "Not bad, right?" He rotated his body to the left (his good side), then pivoted to the right, sucking in his stomach a bit more. "A smartly crafted, day-to-night wardrobe staple," Jimmy said, conjuring the shirt's description as he'd read it on the Nordstrom Rack website. "Subtly tapered to give off a slimming, athletic look."

Jimmy smiled into the mirror, tilting his head to accentuate his jawline, and loving the fact he had such a good memory—better than anyone he'd ever known, in fact. He could recall the price of gas last May 17th, or what he'd had for dinner fifteen Thursdays ago. Jimmy could also access memories from the distant past, like entire days when his mom was still alive or every second he'd spent at Cascade School for Boys.

It was true, his brain was one huge photo album. Some childhood images had aromas attached to them, too, like the smell of his mother's soap as she nestled him against her bathrobe, the reek of teenage boys in proximity, the mingled cloud of a man's coffee breath and cologne inches from his face. Those could hurl Jimmy back without notice, which unfortunately was currently happening. The bathroom had grown freezing. Jimmy squatted and hugged himself, rocking in time to his breath. He had to climb out of the hole again, had to redirect a darkness, that had become such a consumer of his time. He slapped himself hard, which helped, and thought about good things.

So many gifts he had. For instance, there was his semi-professional level—possibly full-on pro—whistling skill. Jimmy was indeed a master whistler, one who had recently taken things to the next level, when 15 years ago, he'd taken 22 hours of over-the-telephone whistling courses. His teacher was a famous Scottish performer who could tell what you were doing wrong without seeing you. By the end of the course, Jimmy had gotten so good the instructor said there wasn't anything left to correct and hung up.

Jimmy thought of his other assets—he had great calves, above average for a 46-year-old man—also a unique aptitude for knowing the time at any moment, give or take seven to ten minutes. To top it all off, Jimmy was a nice guy. At least he thought so. He laughed at people's jokes and acted interested in what they had to say. He asked questions followed by follow-up questions, even when the answers were boring, which they usually were.

This checklist of positivity seemed to have helped. Jimmy took a few deep breaths and stood up. Better. He winked into the mirror, forcing a dry, toothy smile. Tweaking his hairpiece a tick to the left and a nudge down over his forehead, he chuckled, mildly scolding himself for waiting this long to upgrade. This one looked so much more like real hair. His mood lightened; his shoulders dropped.

On the bathroom counter, Jimmy's phone launched into the opening guitar/drum riff of Rush's *Limelight*.

It was Monty. *Be there around 7. U?*

Leaving now. See you there

C U homes.

Monty was usually late, and it was okay. The Trade Winds was filled with friends. He and Monty would meet up eventually. Jimmy tucked his phone into the front pocket of his jeans and flicked off the bathroom light. As he walked, the "zzip" sounds of the new denim rubbing against itself along his inner thigh annoyed him. No problem, the noise level at the Trade Winds would be enough to drown it out. He gave himself a once-over in his bedroom's full-length mirror. "All systems go, Houston." Jimmy grabbed his keys, locked the deadbolt, and broke into the loudest, most pitch-perfect version of *Don't Stop Believin'* his neighbors could ever hope to hear whistled in their hallway. They were welcome.

The restaurant was only a five-block walk from Jimmy's apartment, and well-lit most of the way, but as he made his way into a dark section of sidewalk, his buoyant attitude began to dissolve. Remnants of his recent bout in the bathroom began flaring up inside him. Within seconds, he was back in that dusty, muggy instrument room where he worked after school. It was a closet really—no windows or ventilation. He'd listen for the sounds of a heavy door opening and closing in the distance and of Mr. Johnson, the music director, clearing his throat. The click-clack of dress shoes on the hallway's linoleum floor would signal his rapid approach. Seconds later one of those fancy shoes would thud against the instrument room door, and Jimmy would open the door to reveal his teacher with stacks of sheet music cradled in his arms. The man's facial expression confused Jimmy; it was so much different than the stoic, grumpy disposition he'd display during class. That guy rarely joked or even smiled, but this Mr. Johnson was grinning like a little boy. His giddy, unblinking onceover had terrified and confused young Jimmy. A few folders had fallen from his grasp and onto the floor, sheet music flying everywhere, and that's how it started. "James," Mr. Johnson would say as he closed the door behind him. "I'm afraid I must request your assistance."

As the unlit stretch of sidewalk ended, Jimmy dug a knuckle into his ribs to lift himself out of this unforeseen emotional plunge. He stopped and assessed his reflection in a storefront window—at least he looked good. Following two more positive affirmations and 24 deep breaths (four sets of six), he was again feeling decent as he opened the door to the Trade Winds. Yvette stood at the hostess stand, just to the left of Jimmy's preferred perch by the fire pit. He liked the spot; it gave him a view of the whole place—waiting area, dining room, bar—and less chance of being surprised by anybody.

"How you doin', Jimmy?" said Yvette. "You look nice. New shirt?"

"Hello, Yvette, yes, it's new." He looked down at his wrists. "I like the orange cuffs."

"I do too," she said. "They make you pop."

Jimmy spotted Orlando at the bar, working fast and efficient as usual while still able to joke and chat with people. Two at a time, he set four cocktails on a tray and took a sip of a beverage. "Speaking of pop," Jimmy said, "I could use one myself." Good one, he thought—or maybe said.

"Okay, Jimmy," said Yvette. "Take care, honey."

It always stung a little when people called him "honey." Jimmy's mom had called him that, up until the day she died of cancer in a hospital bed. But how would Yvette know that? Jimmy wasn't offended. Besides, he had a theory Yvette might have a crush on him. There were signs of it—the way her face lit up each time Jimmy showed up in the lobby, how she was always telling him how nice he looked. She might offer a quick glance and smile as she led a group of diners past him. This was fine. He was a single, successful, nice-looking man with decades of experience in the customer service industry. It made sense she would be attracted to him.

Jimmy found an open space at the bar and watched Orlando make Bloody Mary's. Orlando spotted Jimmy and flashed a handsome grin. He whipped a towel over his shoulder and strode over, greeting Jimmy with a hard high five. "What's up, my dude! The usual?"

"Yes. Light on the ice, please."

"Aye, aye, Commodore." Orlando slapped a coaster down and set Jimmy's Coke on it. "Cheers," he said, and disappeared to the other end of the bar. At first, Jimmy had felt rejected when Orlando walked away abruptly like this. One minute they'd be discussing Minecraft and the next, Orlando was gone, filling up a shaker fifteen feet away. Jimmy knew now it wasn't personal, Orlando wasn't being mean or anything. It wasn't in the same ballpark as the pain he'd dealt with at Cascade, at least until Monty came along. Jimmy understood bartending was difficult and hectic like Jimmy's job, and there was no doubt he and Orlando were good friends, regardless of how often they spoke.

Turning his back to the bar, Jimmy was pleased to see his favorite spot by the fireplace still wide open. He strode quickly over, and placed his drink on the slate counter, just as his phone buzzed. Another text from Monty.

Running late. See you when I see you.

OK, Jimmy replied.

Jimmy felt a hand on his shoulder. His head shot around, and the hand quickly retreated.

"Hey, Jimmy. Sorry, did I scare you?"

"Oh, hello, Angela. Yes, uh, no." He exhaled and slouched.

"Happy Tuesday," she said. "How's your week going?"

Jimmy was embarrassed by his clumsy reaction to her gesture. It was a simple shoulder pat, for Pete's sake. He was struck with a sharp urge to adjust his hairpiece, so he pretended to scratch a deep scalp itch that required some digging and regained his composure while tweaking things up top. "Pretty good, I guess. Thank you for asking."

"You're welcome. I like your shirt. Great colors."

Angela was beautiful. To Jimmy, her eyes projected acceptance and love, and made him feel more at ease with her than anyone besides Monty. She wore a ring with a small green stone on her left ring finger, which wasn't a diamond, so Jimmy never knew if she was engaged, married or single. A sharp jolt of adrenaline coursed through him. It couldn't hurt to ask, right? Yes, he would do it, he would ask Angela out, on a date. He felt the moment rising, the words beginning to form in his mouth.

But no. Just stop it. It would be foolish, and he would regret it. Someone always gets hurt. He'd learned time and again relationships amount to pain, and Jimmy had no intention of pulling Angela or anybody else into a world with secrets he could never reveal. For the rest of his life, no one would be allowed in but Monty, and that was fine.

Jimmy took a breath and forced a smile. "Are you working in the bar tonight?"

"No, unfortunately," Angela said. "I'll be in the family section. If people tip decently and I don't get thrown up on, I can deal. Oh hey, someone was asking about you the other day."

"Which day?"

"Saturday."

"I wasn't here on Saturday."

"I know."

"I'm usually here on Tuesdays, Thursdays, Fridays and Saturdays."

"Right."

"But last Saturday I was at the Rotary Club spaghetti dinner fundraiser," Jimmy said. "Only six dollars, including meatballs, unlimited garlic bread and salad with three choices of dressing. Who was asking about me?"

"Emma," said Angela.

"Emma from Thursday night karaoke?"

"That's her. She said she saw you at the Safeway on Roxbury. She didn't know you worked there."

"Oh. Well, I've worked there for over 200 months now." Jimmy drained the last of his watery ice. Time for another Coke.

"I think she was just surprised to see you in a different setting, you know?" Angela reached back and tightened her apron. "You weren't dressed all snazzy like we're all used to seeing you here. You had that whole working man thing going on. She said you looked busy."

Was Emma interested in him too? Nice as she was, he'd already ruled out Angela, who was as close to perfect as anyone could be. There was no question Emma would have to settle for a friendship as well.

"My man!" Monty burst through the door, the evening chill clinging to his leather jacket. He pulled up a stool beside Jimmy. "Good to see you, buddy. Nice shirt! Evening, Angela,"

"Hi, Monty. Well, guys, got to do my rounds. Can I get you something, Monty?"

"I'll have a grapefruit White Claw."

"Coming right up."

"Thanks," said Monty. "So, what's up, *dawg?* Sorry I'm late." Monty draped his jacket over the stool and looked Jimmy up and down. They were dressed nearly identically: multi-colored button-up shirts—Monty's had a paisley pattern—designer jeans and light brown loafers.

"We are looking fly, if I do say so myself," said Monty.

Jimmy leaned into the sound of Monty's voice, his body veering toward it like a flower to the sun. Since the day Monty had arrived at Cascade, he'd been Jimmy's refuge. Jimmy still didn't know why Monty had decided to stick up for him at school, let alone why he'd decided to be his friend. The fact was, he had, but because of that, Monty had paid a price too. The bullies were all sizes and ages, and the adults were usually the worst.

"How's work?" said Jimmy.

"Shitty," Monty said. "Shitty at best. Sheet metal never ceases to be awkward. Whether you're carrying it or cutting it, it's almost impossible to avoid slicing yourself up from handling it the wrong way. Rarely is it a smooth day when working with that shit."

"I know what you mean," said Jimmy. "Most days at Safeway, I'm either cleaning up messes or fetching shopping carts. Bagging groceries is okay, I guess."

"And they let you wear your Seahawks swag to work on game days," Monty said. "Ain't nothing wrong with that labor practice."

"I don't like football."

"Whatever."

Jimmy smiled as he surveyed the crowded restaurant. Sprinkled throughout, among the diners and drinkers and families and one well-behaved dog, was everyone in the world he cared about. Orlando, behind the bar, Yvette at the front greeting all who entered, Angela, lovely Angela, weaving her way through the packed dining room with trays of fish tacos and Mai Tais. And sitting next to him was Monty, one of the two people Jimmy would ever love without barriers. There were so many good people under this single roof. Jimmy licked his dry lips and realized other than his work headaches and occasional dark moments, life was doggone good.

His gaze drifted back to the lobby, where a woman was leading an elderly man toward the hostess desk. She stopped his wheelchair in front of Yvette. The old man positioned just a few feet away, Jimmy took in the man's gray skin and slumped posture. His body projected failing health, but it was something else that drew Jimmy in. A cloud of cologne and mustiness had trailed behind the man, and now occupied the firepit/lobby area.

But it still hadn't registered completely, not until the old man was pushed by Jimmy and their eyes met. Jimmy's mental photo album flew open as his brain took in the data. Abruptly, Jimmy's knees gave out and his elbows slammed into the slate tabletop. His throat was clenched so tight it was nearly closed.

"It's him."

"Dude, what's wrong with your voice?" said Monty.

"It's Mr. Johnson."

"Mr. Who?"

"Mr. Johnson. From Cascade."

Monty's eyes narrowed as he looked at Jimmy. "Bullshit, man. Mr. Johnson's either dead or, like, 200 years old."

"It's not bs, Monty." Jimmy pointed to a table toward the back of the room. "He's over there, with that woman. See him? And he is old. He would be. Look at him."

"But why would Mr. Johnson be hanging out at some random joint like this?"

"We live in Seattle, Monty. The school is seven miles from here, so maybe he's always lived in the neighborhood. Regardless, that's him. He's old now, but I'll never forget the smell and the face."

"I can't tell from here," Monty said, "but let me tell you something: If that motherfucker is still alive, I pray to God that every day of his life is the same fucking torture chamber he created for us. I pray he wears goddamn diapers and he's so goddamn demented he can't process the rules to fucking Candyland. Should I keep going with my wish list?"

Jimmy awkwardly placed a hand on Monty's shoulder. He knew it was probably the right thing to do, but the gesture still felt hollow. Maybe saying something positive would help. "At least he finally stopped."

Monty's eyes glazed over, and he looked away.

"What's wrong?"

"Nothing."

"Monty, I can tell something's wrong. You're crying."

"Forget it," Monty sniffed as he dabbed at his eyes with a napkin.

"No. You need to tell me. I'm your best friend."

Monty stared into the dining room, then returned his gaze to Jimmy. "Mr. Johnson stopped hurting you." Monty stared at the ceiling for what seemed to Jimmy like three minutes, then finally focusing on his friend. "But that doesn't mean he stopped hurting everyone."

"What do you mean?"

Monty scooted his stool closer to Jimmy. "Remember when you told me how he was messing with you every afternoon in the band room?"

"Yes."

"And then one day, he just stopped?"

"Yes."

"Well, he didn't just stop out of the goodness of his heart."

"What do you mean?"

"Let's just say I offered myself up as a substitute," said Monty.

"What?" Jimmy was shaking. "You shouldn't have done that."

"I was tired of seeing you get hurt and doing nothing."

"You were twelve," Jimmy said.

Monty lowered his voice. "It's ancient history. But for old time's sake, I wouldn't mind going over there and having a look for myself. Chances are it's just some generic old white fuck who's worn Old Spice and drank Folgers for the past 80 years like millions of other old fucks. But I'll know him if I see him."

"Wait, Monty," said Jimmy. He could feel something rising inside him. His chest and stomach were warm with adrenaline. "I'll go over there. I need to be the one to do it."

"Do what?"

"This one is mine. I want to be the one protecting you—for once."

Monty exhaled. "Look, brother, I'm touched. I really am. But let's say you walk over there. And let's say it is Mr. Johnson or someone you think is him. Then what? Are you going to grab a steak knife off the table and find out once and for all if he was born without a heart?"

"I just want to look him in the eye," Jimmy said. "I want him to know I'm not a helpless little kid anymore, that I'm not scared of him." Jimmy's heart raced, but he felt energized. "And he can't hurt me anymore. Can't hurt you."

Jimmy's gaze maintained a laser focus on the back of the old man's head.

"Dude," said Monty, "I hate to break this to you, but he's not going to remember either of us. He looked at me with nothing but cow eyes. We were a fucking speck of shit in this guy's life. We were two of, what, thousands?"

"I don't care," Jimmy said, his eyes still affixed to the corner table. The woman now sipped a Margarita and the old man a milkshake. "I'm going over there, alone."

Monty put a hand on Jimmy's shoulder. "Let's be real. You're not going over there. Let it go. We've both moved on. I mean, look at us."

Jimmy inspected himself, then Monty, but nothing about how they looked really registered.

"Not to mention," said Monty, "that shriveled up old fuckstick is destined to die soon, to be followed up with an eternity as Satan's bitch. I say you step back and let nature take its course."

"Okay, the woman just left their table and headed toward the restroom," said Jimmy. "Perfect. I'll be back."

Jimmy sprung off the stool.

"You're making a big mistake," Monty said.

Jimmy ignored Monty and made his way into the dining room. Within seconds, he reached the table and stood behind the old man, staring down at his wispy, white crown. Jimmy felt calm and in control, plus, the man was so preoccupied with his milkshake, he didn't notice Jimmy hovering over him.

"Mr. Johnson?" said Jimmy, gaze locked on the back of the man's head.

"Who's that behind me?" The man gripped his wheels with trembling, bony fingers and lurched diagonally backwards. His napkin dropped off his lap and under the table.

Hefty but not cumbersome, the steak knife balanced nicely in Jimmy's palm. He squeezed the handle lightly while he waited for the man's head to pivot on its ancient neck. Finally, their eyes met.

"I'm terribly sorry," said the old man. "I'm afraid I must request your assistance."

He was the only person Jimmy had ever known who used that phrase, the final instance occurring on March 26, 1990. "No problem," Jimmy said. He knelt in front of the old man, cuffing the knife a few inches from his tormentor's elderly groin. It would be the perfect revenge—to slash, to stab, to mangle the repulsive symbol of his stay at CSB. Jimmy paused briefly and thought about it. He grabbed the napkin and covered the knife with it as he rose to his feet, slicing straight up Mr. Johnson's shin bone with the weapon's toothy edge.

Jimmy slipped the steak knife between his jeans and untucked shirt and looked at Mr. Johnson. The old man apparently hadn't even noticed the assault, or even the blood that was now seeping through his pant leg. His wheelchair was half pointed at Jimmy, but Mr. Johnson's focus seemed distant. He didn't appear to be paying attention to anything. His milkshake was gone, his pant leg was soaking in blood and there was a good chance he wouldn't be around this time next year. That's when Jimmy decided there was no need for a discussion, much less a lecture.

"Mr. Johnson, I don't swear," said Jimmy, flicking a speck of the Trade Winds carpet grit from his new shirt, "but on behalf of Monty and me, fuck you."

"What? I, well, what…" Mr. Johnson stammered.

"Goodbye, Mr. Johnson."

Jimmy turned and left the dining room, picking little pieces of trouser fabric from the steak knife, then dropping it off at a busing station. He strolled up to Monty back at the fire pit.

"So, was it him?" said Monty.

"Yeah. It was him."

"What were you doing under the damn table?"

"Getting his napkin. Then slicing his shin with a steak knife."

"Are you fucking serious?"

"I don't think he even felt it. And I said fuck you from you and me. That was more for you."

"Thanks for that. Did anyone see you?"

"I don't think so. He was sitting there by himself."

Monty put his arm around Jimmy. "Do you feel better now? Now that you've physically assaulted an elderly individual in a goddamn wheelchair?"

Jimmy smiled. "I do, Monty. I do feel better. But I also feel bad about not feeling bad about hurting him. So, both."

"Well, like you said, fuck him," said Monty. "I wouldn't be losing a wink of sleep over committing that minor act of retribution. You must be parched after that shanking. Why don't you get yourself a Coke and we'll lay low for a bit. If anyone starts asking questions regarding Mr. Johnson's accident, we may have to skedaddle."

"Okay."

As Jimmy made his way to the bar, Orlando darted past him, weaving his way into the dining room with a first aid kit under his arm. Mr. Johnson's margarita-drinking companion followed behind, looking angry.

No problem, Jimmy could wait for another Coke. Things felt positive again, just like they'd been before Mr. Johnson was wheeled in. This was Jimmy's home, and in it he'd defended Monty, himself, and everyone he loved against a bad person. His body buzzed. Angela stopped at the firepit, set her tray on the counter, and nodded toward the corner table. "That guy in the wheelchair has a bloody leg. No one can figure out how it happened. He's got dementia."

Jimmy and Monty exchanged looks. But at this point, Mr. Johnson's leg didn't matter anymore, anyway. Neither did Mr. Johnson. Jimmy looked at Angela's hand and the ring she wore every day that may or may not mean anything. He gingerly adjusted his hairpiece and willed himself to look into her eyes.

"Um, Angela, I was wondering…"

POETRY

Now I Know Why Tom and Huck Staged Their Own Funerals

nicholas barnes

got me a mansion of selves bottled up inside. they're having roommate disagreements about libertad again. the palace is on fire. can't do nothin to quell the burning. cause i'm mired in the hell called i. need detention from myself. need hermitage from myself. necesito una separación from myself. asylum from myself. desert island from myself. i wear long hair, denim ball caps, taiwan mnfctrd wayfarers—in hopes of fading in to the fullest extent. i'm a mortar at the county fireworks show. climb to fall. apex to peak. alpha to omega. then start anew. please excuse me, i'm a firefighter, but not by trade or pleasure. i keep putting seasoned madrone on my jack flash coalbed. that is, until the flames die, and i get what i always wanted: to live life in a vacuum. no one will know me. just like that first coat of paint on aunt polly's white picket fence. olvidado.

that's the spirit
elizabeth galoozis

she decided just to haunt
the tool shed.
there was more to rattle:
trowels, rakes, loose screws—
even some chains,
if she was feeling old-school.

the house had become
too mundane.
when they weren't sleeping or gone
they bored her
with their somnolent sameness:
picking their fingers,
chewing,
staring at their screens.

when they come into the shed,
they are more focused:
choosing a blade,
riled up
to build or destroy something.
much more fun, then,
to slip across their wrists
or land a spiderweb strand
on the backs of their necks.
make them look alive.

Poem-Thief

roger camp

for Harry Gordon

I stole a poem once from my dear friend
    whose last words when we departed Nick's on 2nd
were "Don't steal my fuckin' poem."
    I nodded my head in agreement

but outside minutes later,
    the fumes of my gin martini
infused with the exhaust of 2nd St.
    compelled me to think

of a jewel thief,
    a consummate professional
the likes of which were played
    by a Cary Grant or David Niven.

Enticed, I joined their coterie
    and became a poem-thief.
In my mind the crime took place in Nice
    where I slipped into his room

through the open balcony window and nicked his notes
    while he was on the beach ogling a gaggle
of French breasts. I didn't exactly steal the idea
    of how my friend killed a man once

but instead wrote a poem about a reporter
    who made the mistake of a lifetime,
a simple mix up of names which made the papers
    reporting one dead, one alive in a car crash

until twenty-four hour later a correction
    invoked a resurrection.

How Categorical My Variables Were
heikki huotari

Who's on first the chicken or the egg, the flying pie, the memory of money, one of many functions, every hill a hill to die on, ha ha made you look then made you look away. While sighting only kayaks I'm denying stable equilibria. I'm seeing trees of green until the trees of green are fully seen then moving on to roses. Of what state is the paraboloid the flower? Be specific, gravity, with dates and names. The nights are numbered. In the land of the exclusive "or" the man who's evil and incompetent is king. Tent cities are bulldozed, the social problem solved completely. Let me tell you how my bête noir looks and acts and of the color of my bête noir's hair. Look here, say the intelligent designers, If Ben Franklin flies a kite and doesn't die you'll want to too. Blest are involuntary celibates for they'll go forth and multiply. Blest are the single cells for they'll divide. On your investment I'll be the return.

Aglaecwif

cindy veach

Outside my window men are repainting the crosswalk
putting new lines over old lines.

I learned a new word today, an Old English word—
aglaecwif—a monster-woman, troll-lady, wretch, hag.

Think, The Grand High Witch of All The World.
Think, Grendel's no name mother.

And then I learned that this word aglaecwif
is the feminine form of aglaeca: a hero,

a valiant warrior. Why am I not surprised? I know
these tropes: the monster mother, the childless crone—

toothy, bald, clawed, toeless child haters, child eaters.
If all witches are women as Roald Dahl wrote

then I claim that pedigree but explain why gender
makes me witch not warrior, hag not hero. What

patriarchal alchemy creates monsters out of what
I'm supposed to be versus what I am?

I have tried to be good, to exist between the lines
yet look at me, my galaxy of monsters.

*This poem borrows from and was inspired by Susan Rich's poem "Boketto"
and this quote from "Women and Other Monsters" by Jess Zimmerman:
"Monsters are created in the difference between what we are supposed to be
and what we are."*

Cheekovsky the Monkey

chris menezes

My wife was in love with this small stuffed monkey
bought the night of her cancer surgery.
She called him Cheeky.

He was a perfect fit on her stomach,
covered her staples with
a smile of yarn
and dense beady eyes.

I gave him personality
to hear her laugh
from her hospital bed.
He nestled his head
against her shoulder,
rubbed his black leather nose
on her nose, humped her chest
and whacked off with vigorous speed.

On our honeymoon,
we watched *The Fantastic Mr. Fox* from my laptop
as Cheeky slept in between us.

When she realized he was missing,
she slid down to the gum-spotted concrete
of San Francisco, in front of the rental car office,
a river of people flowing by, not noticing.

They found him under the covers,
said they would ship him home.
She couldn't sleep until he was
pressed against her chest again.

He lives in a box now, tucked
between two children's books,
our last sonogram and
an unused onesie.

Pack Wife
isabelle walker

Apropos of carrying things, as in the work of mules and donkeys;
germane to the subject of disregard, my once-husband did not offer
to carry my suitcase across those small intervals of space—front
door to car, car to train, car to airport skycap. At least, not after that
time in our newlywed year when I replied to his offer of help, *It's
okay, I got it!* practicing the stoic virtue I learned growing up, but
unaware I was saying I got it for the rest of our lives together.
Other things he made me shoulder by silently judging not his job
included the saying of no to our toddler's appetite for candy,
television, running with pens, skipping through busy parking lots,
but also my need for holding, understanding, the occasional
hug. While he wafted through decades of marriage weightless as a
hummingbird, dipping into this daylily and that buttercup, I could
barely see the horizon, my spine bent so far over it was parallel to
the ground from the weight of all he would not touch.

Dream

andrew robin

I wanted to be
an astronaut.

But I was timid,
and poor at math.

So they told me to
change my dream.

Now I want to
be an arctic wolf.

The Time-Space Continuum

katherine van eddy

I've found the wormhole, Mr. Hawking,
while you were still thinking
about your party for time travelers
when no one arrived.
On one end is snow
on the other, evergreens:
the years between stretched
just large enough for me to pass through.

Should we consult science or poetry
to understand the way I traveled,
still unable to free myself
from the gravity of his words?

I did not predict we'd keep writing,
our words reaching across time
and space, creating a kind of room
where we leave them, where he and I visit,
but never together. By the time
I read his next letter, he is already gone.
As I stay to write mine, only echoes.

We speak and wait for answers.
Any moment the tunnel could collapse,
a dying star dragging everything
around it into the abyss—
my husband, two children, this self
I barely recognize—
yet I shiver, remembering

his touch, tender fingers
curling my hair behind my ear
as I lay with my head in his lap
while some movie plays for us alone.
Knowing even then it wouldn't last.

NONFICTION

Uses for a Mouth

melody greenfield

> When you see me, I exist.
> – Jeannine Oullette, *The Part That Burns*

I know for certain that, to ring in New Year's 2000, my tenth-grade girlfriends and I took a car service to a house party in LA's deep valley, where every strip mall had a rundown donut store, auto body shops were as common as gas stations, and it was always at least ten degrees hotter than anywhere else in Los Angeles. I also know that there were 100 or 150 kids there—the majority from the four local private schools and a few, like me (as evidenced by our discount purses), from public schools.

Before arriving, we twelve girls, who'd all once attended the same prep school, and still went by the moniker "The Twelve," sat in a circle on our friend Alisa's living room floor and drank. (Her separated folks were away for the evening.) In addition to the liquor we'd scrounged up from our own homes, we helped ourselves to her family's plentiful stash—Absolut, Grey Goose, Ketel One—swallowing shot after unsupervised shot. Shot one: forget I hate my broke, divorcing parents for taking me out of private school. Shot two: forget I hate my pest of a little brother for being Mom and Dad's favorite. Shot three: forget I hate my thighs and how, even at 5'7, 120 pounds, they jiggle when I shake them and wrinkle when I pinch them. We were a good ten shots in before the big white VanGo van pulled up in the circular driveway and *beep-beeped*.

I wish I could recount my night chronologically and explain my actions with clarity and confidence, but I can't. I drank to forget. While I remember pieces of that New Year's, I don't have all of it. In fact, more of it than I'd like to admit is in shadow and in gray, and some of it is just black.

I'm positive about some details. Blurry photos confirm that I wore white jeans and a white halter top, no bra—like a sexy angel, minus her halo—and that I flat ironed my light brown, shoulder-length hair and made it shiny with smoothing serum. I remember, quite clearly, seeing the other girls throughout the evening for a moment here or there—an outstretched hand, an excited squeal, a swig of punch—but then they were gone again, lost among the crowd. The party's playlist left an indelible mark too—

1. Britney or Christina, boyband
2. Jennifer Lopez, boyband
3. Destiny's Child, boyband

—and I have an equally strong memory of the décor. Beer cans spilled out of a giant cooler shoved beneath a foldout table from Costco, on top of which sat different-flavored Jell-O shots in Tupperware containers, oversized jugs of cheap vodka, Solo cups, and a fruity, red chaser. But, somewhere between Jell-O Jigglers and Jenny from the Block, I ended up on my knees, performing fellatio on five near-strangers—only three of whom I can partially recall. Grainy snapshots, fuzzy and fragmented, are all I'm left with: a floating piece of conversation here; a patch of wet grass there; the feeling of cold tile against my fair, goose-pimpled skin; the rare, surprising sound of my own laughter; the sour smell of Leah vomiting into her Kate Spade bag; crumpled lace underwear at the foot of a bed.

When I replay that night in my brain like a pixelated movie and watch myself go through the motions with these young men—in the side yard with Josh the Jock, in the bathroom with Catholic School Boy, and in the kitchen with someone forgettable and monosyllabic (Matt or Mike?)—it's like I'm watching someone else draw them in close, kiss their lips, unzip their pants. *Is that really me? You would never do that*, I think. And yet, I did.

It's been over twenty-three years since then. The wide-eyed girl I see faintly in my mind's eye isn't present-tense me, and she's got the missing crow's feet to prove it. Still, I recognize those sad blue eyes, the freckles that dot her worried face, the asymmetrical breasts, and the bravado that masks so much insecurity, and I feel protective of her, as if she were my little sister.

When I took Josh's hand that New Year's Eve and pulled him to the side of the house before pulling down his pants, the party, like his dick in my mouth, was growing. Josh was an attractive athlete whom I knew peripherally from the private school scene, even though for the past two years, I felt as if I'd been slumming it at my neighborhood public school: a mediocre place named after a mediocre president. It was maddening to me that my parents, who now kept separate residences, could no longer fake their keeping-up-with-the-Joneses charade. Like them, I wanted to be fancy and fit in—all of us Greenfields scrambling for acceptance in a world where we were outsiders. (A world with the designer handbags I coveted.) Teens of means, most of my fellow celebrants lived in an out-of-reach financial stratosphere, but tonight I happily, and very visibly, circled within their orbit.

"Melody, people can see us," Josh worried aloud. He turned his back to a group of drunken partygoers, but I kept going, unfazed, my head bobbing up and down between his strong yet slender soccer-player thighs as his soft, dark leg hairs tickled my face. Had it not been for the details of my grass-stained knees and his hiding from passersby, Josh, with his good looks and popularity, might have helped to boost not only my ego, but also my social standing. Instead, the incidents of the evening would amount to social suicide, but I didn't know this yet.

There were sexual mores we high schoolers implicitly understood and consented to. Kiss someone random at a party?—no problem. Try oral with your significant other in private?—sure. But Josh was an acquaintance at best, and everyone was watching. My all-white outfit may have hinted at purity, but my actions said otherwise. My sins were on full display. For the moment though, none of that, not even our audience, mattered, as I focused on the singular task of giving my first-ever blowjob. *Slippery*, I remember thinking of Josh's penis, wet with my saliva, and then everything goes hazy.

My next flash of memory has me in a half-bath/powder room with some dude from one of the nearby parochial schools. I don't know his name or what he looked like—just that his cock was a beige Tootsie Roll in my mouth. I told him as much, then chuckled into his pint-sized package. This kind of mean-spirited mocking is called negging, and, at fifteen, I did a lot of it, passing off as humor the same misplaced cruelty I faced at home. *Fuck you*, Catholic School Boy rightly replied when I didn't even have the decency to feign sarcasm or backtrack with an *I'm kidding*.

I'm told I blew a boy in the kitchen next, quite publicly. Someone named Jon or Jeff? Dave or Dan? All I can recall is a window above the sink with creamy yellow curtains and the smell of lemon dish soap mixing with another less pleasant aroma: something akin to a foot trapped in a sock. Was I close to blacking out, or did I disassociate? Was it the stench of an old sponge I caught a whiff of, or was it Jim's/Tim's/Tom's sweaty balls? Assuming he finished, perhaps the odor I'm remembering is semen, which I've since learned can be as thin and tasteless as water or as thick and heavy as spoiled cream and reek of fermentation, à la hearts of palm—a pickled pleasure, despite how its smell turns my stomach.

Without my own solid memories or social media to turn to, I've had to rely on secondary sources, like my friends, for answers. While they were also intoxicated, they were more lucid than I was, and they've corroborated seeing me in action, all telling some version of the same story: *We tried to stop you. We attempted to reason with you. But you'd already made up your mind.* By their accounts, I was as drunk on power as I was on Smirnoff. I bulldozed my way in.

I don't need anyone's help fleshing out this next part; I have a mental picture of it. There was a late-20s, pseudo-chaperone present—the aunt of the boy hosting. She was kind and patient and wore suit pants, and she was trying to keep me safe while I sobered up. I can still hear her now. "Lie down. Sleep it off," she said, but I was belligerent and didn't listen to her because here was my free pass to unleash on an authority figure. Plus, I was convinced I knew better than she did.

"I'm gonna fingerbang you!" I warned her, to which she laughed, but I didn't. Despite the Prozac of my youth, and the other brands of antidepressants I'd try in the years to come, I was the Fiona Apple of my friend group: the "Sullen Girl" not easily moved to happy overtures. I didn't finger her either; drunks have poor follow-through. Sloppy and unintelligible, I turned my attention to someone more age-appropriate: Sara, the coolest girl in our grade.

Earlier in the evening, Sara and I had jokingly promised each other that if we didn't "hook up," we'd kiss each other. We both did hook up with guys at the party, or in her case, guy singular, but we were so wasted, we made out in plain view of ogling onlookers anyway. "We pinky swore," I slurred, before moving our girl-on-girl private party into one of the empty bedrooms.

When I revisit this moment in my mind, we're on a bed, and I'm taking off her panties. I think about licking her *down there* but panic, even though this isn't the first time I've been with a girl. Nevertheless, and despite having girl parts of my own, the mechanics of female anatomy make me anxious. Unlike giving blowjobs, which, as of tonight, has become second nature to me, I haven't the faintest idea where to start with a same-sex act I've never performed, so, instead, I continue tongue-mouthing Sara until we both pass out, cold.

> Lemme throw it into reverse.
> – Lidia Yuknavitch, *The Chronology of Water*

As a child, I desperately craved attention because it was in short supply. My parents each worked more than full-time jobs with Dad driving an hour away to his photo shop business six days a week and Mom pulling double shifts as a home economics teacher and caterer. They hustled but were still strapped for cash, and not just because they liked the finer things in life. My little brother Seth, 18 months my junior, had special needs, including Autism and ADHD, in addition to a host of other medical problems stemming from being a preemie. Between surgeries and therapies, Seth's care wasn't cheap. Strained finances accounted for most of Mom and Dad's fights, and all the arguing further distracted them.

I learned early that when it came to the spotlight, even as I knew Seth rightfully demanded more of my parents' time and energy, I could either put on living room shows, singing and dancing and pretend-playing the guitar, or I could act out: testing limits, talking back, and serving up all the snark and sass I could muster. Naturally, I checked all these boxes. I was always finding new ways to be noticed too: student-of-the-year trophy, eating disorder, sexual experimentation—check, check, check.

As my body shrank, Dad's temper flared. "Watch your tongue!" he snapped if he didn't like the words I said or the tone I used. When he punished me by calling me names or washing my mouth out with soap, the message was clear: my mouth was as bad as I was. "You don't have to listen to her, Seth. She's a witch," he'd say. Or, when I went on one of my cleaning sprees, furiously washing dishes and taking Windex to all the glass surfaces in the house until they sparkled and shined, it was, "You're sick. You have a problem." A few times, he slapped me across the face for the way I spoke to Mom, and once he even hit me with his belt for talking back to him when he suggested my shorts were too short. "You belong on Sunset Boulevard," he said, implying I was dressed like a hooker. The truth was, I was slimming down, and now that people were finally taking notice, including friends' leering fathers, concerned teachers on the schoolyard, and my classmates, who all wrote as much in my sixth-grade yearbook, I wanted to show off.

I remember being 11 and standing on the front lawn when one of my mother's catering friends came by to help us set up for a garage sale. "Look at you, skinny minny!" she smiled approvingly at my willowy figure. What a relief! Her comment meant I was starting to look less like Mom, whose pear-shaped body I hated with the same intensity I'd begun to hate my own. At the time, the sight of Mom's bulging bottom made me ill enough to puke. But this moment was confirmation that the jumping jacks I'd been doing at recess, in lieu of eating lunch, were paying off and that even if Dad thought I was rotten at my core, at least it was getting more defined. (Thank you, decreasing body fat and never-ending crunches!) That my ribs were sticking out was simply an added bonus.

Rewind to age ten though, and you'd find me eating whatever anyone fed me and then some. My meal choices were delicious and vast and often included fancy, refined options for my palate—more mature than its years like precocious, older-looking me. "She's such a good eater," grown-ups regularly commented, as I wolfed down spicy lamb chops I deemed *picante*, all manner of sushi (including raw quail eggs), "exotic" dishes like Moroccan chicken, and caviar I'd sneak on a spoon like it was nut butter. At my yearly checkups, this overindulgence showed. I consistently weighed in at the 90th percentile, where, thankfully, I likewise measured on the corresponding height side of the doctor's chart. I can still see my pediatrician circling the 90s on his page in loud, red marker before closing the folder marked "Melody" and filing it away alphabetically. And thus began a lifelong obsession with numbers that would later translate into my tracking everything from calories and pounds to bedfellows.

It was terribly unfair, meanwhile (or so the jealous child-me thought), that my brother, born prematurely, was naturally skinny like Dad. And Ritalin just compounded this. Regardless of how much In-N-Out Burger my parents force-fed him, Seth never saw any 90s on his medical charts, or on his school papers.

When I think about all the factors that led me to New Year's 2000 and beyond, I think about dual, dueling Melodies. A walking contradiction, I was two things, two people, at once: a waif who felt fat, a perfect student but imperfect daughter and sister. This binary was reinforced by fairy tales and the Bible and even showed up when playing pretend with my brother. When I was nice, I was Good Fairy. When I inexplicably turned mean, I'd been overtaken by the bad one. An enigma, I could love God in one breath—"good Jewish girl" that I was—and let boys feel me up at synagogue in another.

Split me in half, and there was Good Melody with the neatest penmanship and the straightest posture. She was the author of the most polished essays, who never challenged authority, save for her own parents and one undeserving party chaperone. This Melody excelled in English, languages, music, and, with the help of tutors, math and science too. She was the people-pleasing version of me I took to friends' houses, where, neat freak that I was, I always did the dishes, including ones I hadn't dirtied, before moving on to empty their dishwashers or fold their laundry. Then, there was Bad Melody, who got her mouth washed out by her father and used that same mouth, years later, to fellate boys. *You're amazing*, they'd rave. *Keep going*. I craved praise, and their reassurances were a balm.

When I cleaned homes that weren't my own, my motivations were no different. I was after the very approval I sought at school, where there were never enough *good jobs!* to go around. Compliments were my nourishment. Insecure, I hoarded them like I'd once hoarded mashed potatoes. "You act as though you'll go hungry, Mel," my bewildered mom mused at mealtime, back when I still ate. "Chew. Slow down," she urged me, reminding, "there's plenty for everyone."

But I always wanted more: dinner, recognition, love. And all my parents ever seemed to notice was my bad attitude or my sadness, for which they began medicating me in the fifth grade, as my weight and their marriage were first sinking. (Their divorce, due to an endless loop of splitting up and reconciling, took years to stick.)

"Are you sure this is the same person we live with?" Mom would ask my teachers whenever they insisted I was "such a pleasure to have in class!" because the daughter she and Dad knew was entirely different. Their Melody, Bad Melody, wasn't a pleasure but a terror. She was a tantrum-throwing toddler whose favorite word was *No*; a little girl who'd inch one toe and then a whole foot out her bedroom door whenever she was "out of control" and on a time-out, which was often; and an entitled brat who refused to share her colored pencils with her brother.

By middle school, my meltdowns were giving way to newfound rebellions like suggestive photoshoots. Always pushing boundaries, my 12-year-old girlfriends and I, doing our best impression of *sexy*, dressed up in barely-there outfits and took pictures of one another: shoulders exposed, hips cocked, mouths agape. Junior high was also when I started to explore my sexuality more overtly—first, second, and third bases reached with various schoolboys we "Twelve" shared the way we did lollipops. We normalized this incestuous partner passing as if spit-swapping were as ordinary as a trip to the movies, although, by the eighth grade, moviegoing was frequently a co-ed adventure that involved fingers in more places than popcorn. Orgasms were wonderful and transportive, but, while I never admitted as much at the time, being wanted felt better than getting off.

Come high school, I was fully embracing the latest "bad" version of me, akin to the leather-pants-wearing, Danny-Zuko-dating version of Sandy in *Grease*. Underneath my skin-tight, low-cut clothes though—the same ones I teased off in service of the male gaze—I was still closer to the honor-roll achieving, poodle-skirt-and-sweater-clad Sandy. I stayed away from cigarettes and drugs and, my senior year, made valedictorian. Yet, everything I did, from being the teacher's pet to engaging in heavy petting, I did to be seen—a need both bottomless and inexhaustible.

I have heard it said that attention is a form of prayer, and I agree; it feeds our souls. Perhaps the desire to be paid attention to, though it's quieted from a holler to a hum, fuels me as I retell my story now—my *notice me, notice me!* drive as unquenchable as my former sexual one.

It must have been 3 or 4 a.m. when I woke up equally unquenchable at Alisa's on New Year's Day. *Ice. I need ice*, I thought. My friends were in various stages of sobriety and unrest on the couches and floor, and—parched—I stumbled over them and into the kitchen, stabilizing myself with arms outstretched like I was walking on a balance beam, which is exactly how this felt. I hoped ice would not only hydrate me, but also soothe me the way my beloved pacifier once had. The way five cocks had not.

That *whoosh* of cold freezer air—*bam!*—brought me back into my body and the moment, jolting my memory. I held onto the counter to brace myself. *Shit.* Suddenly, it felt like someone had been kicking me in the temples. A hangover, I deduced. Maybe drinking caused nightmares too. Yes, that had to be it. The blowjobs, the almost-cunnilingus, the unaccounted for chunks of time. I got a sick feeling in the pit of my stomach, and it wasn't just the bile that was rising. "Tell me it was just a bad dream," I said to no one in particular—already flashing-forward to what this would mean for me when school resumed, post-winter break, on Monday. A few girls, sensing my worry, shook their heads at me as though in apology. "Sorry, Mel." I placed an ice cube on my tongue and sucked hard. If only I could likewise melt away. My own deepest wish—to be seen—had been granted, but at what cost?

Despite my childhood obsession with do-overs (*Gimme one more chance!* I'd plead during tantrums), and even despite the good fortune that I never became a meme, thanks to when I came of age, I was branded a "slut" for the rest of high school. That hateful, four-letter word was a thought bubble, a picture frame, a title, permanently fixed above me.

Have you ever tried erasing something on a whiteboard but found—no matter the technique you use or the pressure you apply—the writing remains visible? That's how it is with bad reps too. Mine lingered like cloying department store cologne. Yet, as awful as the whispering, the pointing, and the staring felt, and as surprising as this may sound, I didn't judge myself. It was heartbreaking that my reputation stank and stuck and disappointing to learn that do-overs were a thing of fantasy, but I didn't feel ashamed. I felt a rush of endorphins. And, since binging is the yin to starving's yang, this was true when I found myself overeating too—largely it was fun, until it wasn't.

The euphoria I found behind closed bedroom doors, or wide-open, house-party kitchens for that matter, was more addicting than I anticipated. It was better, in fact, than cleaning, starving myself, acing tests, and people-pleasing put together. *This feels good. Keep going*, my developing brain urged me. So, it's no surprise, really, that after one taste, I kept going back for more: one blowjob, two blowjobs, three, four, five. To this day, I became a greedy houseguest on Thanksgiving—one helping, two helpings, three, four, five—heaping all the fixings onto my plate as if so much stuffing will fill a void. As if it won't hurt, and I won't pay a price, later. *There's enough to go around*, I hear my mother's voice reverberating in my skull.

What embarrassed me came after ingesting too much: the bloated, distended stomach, the greasy aftertaste, the burning in my chest and throat, the jeans that might not zip, the scale dial's pernicious upward tick. Or, in this case (from December 31st of '99 and beyond), the way my peers looked at me, with pity or disgust, and how they snickered behind my back and, sometimes, even in front of my face. Although no one I went to high school with was at that party, word of my wildness spread. My classmates' changed perception of me, more than my behavior itself, was what I wished I could take back.

In the aftermath of New Year's 2000, it was finally my chance to fully embrace and embody the Bad Melody that some, including my own parents, had believed me to be all along. As a kid, I'd performed in choruses and talent shows, so playing a role and committing to it came naturally to me. To get into *this* character, whom I sometimes still inhabit, I needed a drink or two. So, though I can't recall all of what went through my head as I gave all that first-time head, I can see the different bathroom floors on the different debauched nights that followed, when I was repeating the same dangerous and adult-beverage-fueled sexual patterns. Until I met my now-husband, months shy of my thirty-first birthday, the high of calling the shots, of feeling desired—even if *tolerated* is really the better word choice—became for me a favorite song I kept rewinding and replaying: repeat, repeat, repeat. Another wayward glance, another knowing nod, another we-understand-one-another, follow-me wink. I was holiday-dinner insatiable.

If this were fiction, and I could go back to New Year's morning, I'd rewrite the scene. I wouldn't worry about my imminent grounding from coming home hungover. I wouldn't worry about what other people thought or might think because, so what? Plenty of my peers and their parents, due to the revealing way I dressed, had made hurtful judgments about me years before this, so why fret now? Instead, I'd set my worries aside—and not in the misguided, alcohol-induced way I'd done the night before, either. In my revision, I'd forget about all that plagued me, from my reputation to my imagined cellulite; I'd forget about hoping to melt away, even as I just as fervently hoped to be noticed; and I'd use this as an opportunity to make an intentional shift, transforming my mouth into a beacon for others—from strangers to my own family members. Perhaps, I'd save a few nice words for myself too.

Or maybe, that's not quite right. Maybe, this is where I'd put the Good Melody/Bad Melody binary to rest and give myself permission to be one united, complicated but whole Melody. Placing that ice cube on my tongue, I'd suck hard and hope harder for the strength to use my worn and weathered lips in a more realistic fashion—a nuanced, both/and fashion. My prayer: *May I use my mouth not only to spurn or hurt or offer services, but also to encourage, support, and love.*

Maybe, to hell with fiction. Maybe, I don't need a do-over at all. Maybe, my mouth is free to just be: power, magic, bitch, or balm. Maybe, it can wrap itself around bodies it has every business and no business wrapping itself around. Maybe, I can use it in any way I choose—to sing or whisper, speak and shout, smile or kiss, utter truths and lies, regurgitate information or food, sip and slurp, spit or swallow. Maybe, I can suck and suck and burn shit to the ground. Maybe, I have. Maybe occasionally, I still do. Maybe, while the uses for a mouth are complex, the truth is simple.

Maybe, Messy Melody is, and has always been, enough.

The Space Explorers

eric p. mueller

Countless cosmic events that shaped the universe as we know it have gone on unnoticed, and I can say I've been a part of at least one of them. It started on the first week of my twenty-fifth year around the sun, and it continues to echo through space. How lucky I was to enter this new astronomical era exploring other worlds, light years forward from all my other experiences.

I had spent New Year's Eve that year bar-backing at the gay club I worked at, one of the most infamous clubs in the world, walking past countless embraces. I broke more than a sweat, picking up empty plastic cups all night, some filled with vomit because of all the partying. For six hours of work, a couple hundred dollars in cash in addition to hourly pay felt like gold, but even though I was surrounded by people, I felt solitary.

Just a year prior, I spent that couples' holiday at my parents' home where I still lived. Spending the ultimate party holiday/couple's holiday alone always felt like a shortcoming. It was great to spend time with my mom. We were still mourning my dad, who's death was fresh for both of us. I spent the night finishing applications to faraway grad schools, scanning gay hookup applications with a profile that didn't show my face.

After soaring to San Francisco, I was pursuing art and a career, not coaching football at my old high school, and working a part-time retail job. I also sustained myself with a job at the school library, teaching, and at a sticky neon gay bar. I'd never been so busy and also in a position to go on a date with a man without the entire town knowing about it. I could finally be out, and it was huge.

But I had no one to kiss at midnight. The most popular gay bar in the country, and no one wanted to make out. While I did kiss my coworker on the cheek after he pulled the rope for a balloon drop, I wanted to be tongue-deep, like so many men around me, that I wasn't affected by the popping balloons around us. Multiple people had told me I was playing things too safe, but I wanted something special.

After the holiday marking the end of the holiday season, I started to pressure myself.

The night of the astronomical incident there was an early screening of *The Downton Abbey* movie at the Castro Theater. I took pictures of myself with the cardboard cutouts of the show's characters to post online. "See? Look how exciting my life is now." At work that night, I backed with two other barbacks who hated each other, so I served as liaison between the two.

The night raged on and was as any other night would be, but a little busier than usual. Collecting glasses off the floor, I imagined my ribcage squeezing like a rat to get through the crowd. Later I'd be told, from regular-sized barbacks, the crowd would always move for me because I was big. The DJ spun his Britney's, Nicki's, Beyonce, Gaga, Katy, Taylor, Ari's, hits from the 90s. Pours were heavy, and glasses were everywhere; everyone seemed to be having a great time. It wasn't any different from New Year's Eve or literally any other night there.

About halfway through, I passed by a man who looked more out of it than the rest of the crowd. It wasn't uncommon for one to five people to get kicked out on a busy night in the Castro. His state of mind was a planet in alignment with its whole system. I'm sure the guy didn't elbow me intentionally, but his elbow did hit my forearm, causing me to drop a glass or two. Before I could even find a broom, some blonde came up to me. *Hey that guy has had way too much to drink. He keeps touching everyone. You gotta 86 him.* The drunk person was kicked out and I found a broom.

Most of the shards of glass made it into the dustpan when I finally put my head up after hearing three or four loud, almost aggressive, *thank yous*. It was the blonde guy from earlier. I'm sure plenty of broken glass shards stayed on the ground and would look like icicles on the floor after closing. In the space between the dance floor and the patio, it was like the lights from both rooms were colliding to create a spotlight just for me and him.

His face reminded me of an English Bulldog/Pit mix: happy to see me but a little tired. His hair was a perfect high fade, short. Blonde, almost as tall as me. His blazer popped among tank tops, but he wasn't the only nicely dressed man there. Had it been a few days ago, I probably would have said "fine" and walked off.

The blonde guy thanked me again, and I looked around the room. Was the bar busy enough that I could get away with talking to him? Only one way to find out.

Thank you. I would have headbutted that guy and split my head open. "Well, I would have gotten you a band aid." I doubted my ability to flirt or that my looks were desirable.

You work too hard. Was this a chance to flirt? I usually never talked to anyone for this long.

"Thanks. I try not to get fired." I went on to say. I take myself seriously, no matter what it is I'm doing.

What else do you do? This can't be the only thing you've got going on. "I study writing. Nonfiction."

His bulldog eyes widened a little, drawing me into his gravitational pull. He smiled for a second, then looked like he was thinking.

I went on to say I write research-driven pieces, too bashful to say I wrote memoir. I looked at the bar again, saw empty glasses shining like crystal amid sweaty bodies.

He said he was going to leave. Maybe he'd see me later.

He did come back and told me he'd came back just to stand on the patio with a glass of club soda and talk to me. He informed me he was trying to hook up with some straight couple that night, but they had a gremlin of a gay friend who c-blocked him. He called him a bitter bottom. *I don't like gremlins. I like guys like you.* Smooth. I melted into a Jello pool. Uncharted territory, countless frontiers.

I did a sweep for glasses every now and again, but the night had calmed down enough, and I wouldn't be able to do closing things until people left, so I was free to get to know him better. *What do you write about?* "Football."

His face tilted to the side and lit up when I mentioned football.

"I played in high school and throughout college on a Division III team. Even coached afterwards." I wanted to mention my dad, who was dead, but I didn't want to kill the mood.

We mentioned places we'd lived: *Sacramento,* "Connecticut," *South Dakota,* "New Jersey," *Korea,* "Pennsylvania," and *Kuwait.* He was in the military. *What brought you out here?* The disco ball in the room next to us and shined its own little glow. "I was sick of the snow and this school said yes." *It's not even that warm here.* We stood so close to each other I could appreciate how much his shoulders stretched his sweater's fabric. He held a blazer in one of his arms.

As the DJ declared it last call, the smiling blonde guy started going on about serendipity. *So, when you're a famous writer one day, how are we gonna' keep in touch?* The patio had gotten cold, and my hands were wet from work. He offered me his number. I prayed I entered it right.

"The military guy?" Ricardo, the doorperson and my good friend, raised an eyebrow and rolled an eye my way. "I read his ID, it was Johnny or Joe or something. Just promise me you won't give a fuck about him. Don't do it." My ears perked when I heard military. Ricardo never said "don't," but he truly did.

I told everyone I still talked to—outside of family—about this exchange. My new SF friends were excited for me, enjoying what one called green excitement. One told me I seemed naïve, and I didn't know what she meant. I talked about everything with him: books, football, music, men. Soon, we made plans for a date next time he was in town. This was the first time I found someone in the wild, no sites or apps.

We planned to spend a Saturday together in two weekends. I don't know why I didn't just take the night off work. It's hard to stop working when you're doing so much of it. When date day came, I wore a navy-blue sweater with a high collar and large buttons which showed just enough chest. We met at a gas station near my place around lunchtime.

He got out of his car, wrapped his arms around me, and gave me a kiss on the cheek. He wore a maroon newsboy hat and matching pants. Part of me wondered if he was the devil, because who else could look good in a maroon newsboy hat and matching pants?

Then he opened the passenger door for me, the one thing my mother told me I needed to do if I ever took a girl on a date. I couldn't tell you what kind of car it was, but I remember it had rolldown windows. We drove to a Taqueria in the Sunset. He was so chatty, a trait shared by most of my early boyfriends and best guy friends. I rarely thought I had anything to say. We talked more about football, about how it's been moving to San Francisco, his military career, writing.

After a post-lunch drink, he asked if I wanted to go to the beach and I said yes. We drove down Judah, dodging the N Train and traffic lights. The closer we were to the beach, the less there was to see in front of us, so by the time we made it, there was only me, him, and fog. I swear it got dark by 2:45 pm in January, especially if I closed at the bar the night before. Winter was odd in the Bay because you didn't measure the season by how cold or wet it was, but by how close or far the planet is from the sun.

It was too windy and cold even for my sweater. So, we stood close to each other to stay warmer. He checked his trunk for something that'd fit my torso. Before walking to the beach, he pulled out a football jersey. One of his, from a flag league or something. The name on the back read "Jetpack #86."

We didn't take our shoes off. I watched enough true crime to be scared in these moments, but you can't tell me he wasn't about to give me a beautiful first kiss. Instead, he asked me about my dad. Specifically, he asked how he died; "Cancer. Laryngectomy, a stoma." He held on to my hand for a while, we looked out toward the horizon, who knew what lay beyond the ocean's thick fog. *Mine got a big promotion, choked on something later that night while he was celebrating. I was eight.*

I had such a hard time talking about my dad. Writing about it was easier. He had no idea how cool it was for him to ask about it. We were two ex-football players standing at the world's edge, talking about dead dads, and holding hands.

Yet, we did not kiss. A gentleman. He got me home before work. We listened to his mix CD which included "Footloose" and "I Need a Hero." I miss mix CDs. I kicked myself for choosing a date with a time limit. The Castro had come alive while we were out, queers moved up and down the streets like oxygen. A street performer strummed a guitar and played a familiar tune outside my place. Still a gentleman, he walked me to my apartment, and told me he had such a great time. *I like this.* He pointed at my heart. *This.* He touched both of my temples with his thumbs. And I really like this. His fingertips traced veins all the way down my shoulders.

He asked if he could kiss me and moved in for it when I nodded. The streetlights and neon blushed as bright as I did, like an outer planet. I didn't want to bid farewell, but I nearly flew up the stairs to my apartment to change. I was trying to figure out what song the man was playing outside, and deciphered: "I guess this is growing up." It was "Dammit," Blink 182. I was not falling in love, just learning about it. This was growing up, I guess.

My elation continued for the next few days. I wanted to know everything about him. I'd always wanted a Jetpack. How fitting for this man to make my large body feel weightless. I started putting those nonfiction research skills to work, obsessing over him like I was Nick Carroway in *The Great Gatsby*. Or like Gatsby himself. Whatever it was, it reminded me how in Connecticut, I'd park my car in the marina's lot and watch a buoy's green light blink on and off. I was still the young man with tears in his eyes reaching out for sacrosanct green.

Finding his social media wasn't hard but finding out he had a separate life outside of me was. I didn't know the exact details about his life or family, but I did realize I was being foolish in how hard I was crushing on someone I barely knew. To my surprise, he had a past, his own history. The world did not revolve around me. I forced myself to stop researching what to wear to a military ball.

It didn't take long to flip from *Gatsby* to *Jane Eyre*; Jane finding out about Bertha, and I felt the shock that she felt. Or I felt like Bertha herself in *Wide Sargasso Sea*. There was no nonfiction for what I was dealing with. His story was not my story, and we wouldn't ever be equals.

I felt betrayed. He did come by the bar once or twice and left quickly after flirting with me. But seeing him would just make me angry. I'm pretty sure he started having someone check to see if I was working before stopping by.

We had one more date. It was when my mom was in town in early Spring. He sent me a text asking where I was and that he was in the city. His "eyes" saw I wasn't at the bar working. Was I being watched? I would never ditch my mom, but I needed closure.

I took Mom to an Italian restaurant, and we saw *Cinderella*, the one starring Lily James, at a nearby theater. I love that adaptation. All the colors, the waltz choreography. I wanted to tell Mom everything about this Jetpack guy, but I wasn't out to her yet. Even in the 2010s, I was worried it'd sever our relationship.

I met Jetpack at Jane Warner Plaza after I dropped Mom off at her hotel. Walking up Castro Street's hill, I could see the outline of his face from afar looking down and inhaling a cigarette. The night was foggy, so the only lights around us were artificial. He greeted me with a hug and hailed a cab. He opened the door for me. I think he just wanted a peek at my butt.

We went to a piano bar I had never been to. Karaoke for the rich and gray-haired, people sang songs, usually from musicals, accompanied by piano. Jetpack suggested the lemon drop martini. I get it anytime I go back. The bar's tables and chairs were so close together I couldn't get by without my hips bumping into a person or a thing.

A table of women started talking to us. Of course, he can't go anywhere without getting flirted with, I thought. He commented on how great I looked that night and rubbed my shoulder, making me feel uncharacteristically happy and at ease.

Jetpack sang a song from the 1940s. I wish I remembered the title or a lyric to try and find more meaning to him, but I had melted. A man came up to flirt with him afterward and he started to trace my palm with his fingers. We talked about everything from grad school to writing to Cinderella to the growing displays of outrage in Ferguson.

I wanted to tell him more about my dad, how in third grade he got a new job and lived five hours away from us for a year and it felt like I had divorced parents, even though I didn't know what it meant because I only saw him every other weekend. I wanted to see how he'd react to that, but the words stayed behind my quiet lips.

He also mentioned a former Denver Bronco, an offensive lineman, who sometimes got drunk and sent him depressing text messages. Did he seek out types like me? Did he know that I was only a few months off from doing that to him? I'm sure he wasn't mean-spirited. Still, I worried I was being fetishized and not liked for being myself.

A group of women sat behind us. One dropped their phone in front of him. It felt like she was trying to flirt with him, and it made me sad to think someone could "take" a person through interruption like that. He introduced her to me and put his arm around my shoulder. He may have been sketchy, but he knew how to be a great guy.

Maybe he saw my discomfort, but he asked me if I wanted to go anywhere else. I told him I just wanted to go around with him, maybe somewhere we could dance. We made our way back to the main strip and I saw him closely inspecting the front windows of each place we walked by. He settled on a bar not there anymore; one that always had armed security.

I think I paid his cover. The room was so dark and there was enough space even I could shake my booty with only minimum concern I'd look like I was starting a mosh pit. We grinded, we kissed, we held each other and floated. I swear the world around us was spinning while we held each other close and still. His hands went everywhere and when we weren't kissing, we were all teeth grins.

Countless green dots swirled around us, especially along his face. We were back in *Gatsby*, and I was no longer sitting in a parking lot looking at distant blinking buoys. I was a space explorer. There would always be time between us, in addition to the rest of space outside of me. I see the lighting effect at clubs, weddings, bowling allies, and I think of him.

The lights undimmed at last call. *I guess it's time to turn back into a pumpkin.* It stung to hear him say it, but he wasn't wrong. We winced at each other before linking hands. I walked him back to his car, to an obscure side street. We held hands the whole walk and we kissed again while his front door was open. *Thanks for being my hero tonight.* My heart was a pile of breadcrumbs blowing in the wind when the door of his car closed, and my eyes could only see grayscale portraits as I turned around to see the lights had turned off for the night.

The next morning, I saw two bartenders I worked with in matching sweat suits looking like powerwalking housewives. Hardly a hello, they wanted to know who the blonde I was with last night. One said we looked nice together. I had no words, no glass slipper or satellite image. I said, "Someone I shouldn't have been with," and they gasped. Spending the day with Mom was fun, but I wanted to tell her everything and give her a hug.

A friend who studied Brit Lit/the Victorian era consoled me a bit. She said dancing was basically a stand in for sex, for your relationship, anything there isn't enough word space for or that they just can't show. In a matter of months, I'd find my first great love, and he'd be really cool but also an even bigger mess. The universe had been created, but intelligent life was still far off.

Not love, and not even a perfect illusion of it, I was proud of myself for finally taking a giant leap for mankind despite the hurt I was feeling. I cried for him at first, conflating his situation with injustice or malintent towards me. One slow night at work, Lady Gaga's "Marry the Night" came on our many video screens. I walked up to one of the monitors and touched its screen as if it would cleanse me somehow.

With little to hang my hat on, I thought of the younger version of myself who'd much rather be heartbroken than alone, feeling more broken in a general sense. Pride is otherworldly. I didn't just unearth a man or love's endless feeling of light, but a new world entirely. Finally ready to explore space, I didn't realize a small step really could be a giant leap.

Break the Chain

beck m. weiser

I've been told my entire life I'm my mother's mirror image. She has blue eyes just like every TV mother, and light blonde hair, with slight beach waves. When she turned fifty, she started wearing wire-framed glasses, making her look kind. As a teenager, she was a beauty queen who drove her Mustang too fast. She was what every boy wanted and what every girl wanted to be.

I was a scruffy-looking teenager. My hair was blond in the right light, but nowhere near the white blonde she maintained with care in the late seventies. I wore big square-framed glasses glued to my face during fifth grade and never came unstuck.

It was obvious to everyone I was her mirror image, but I was irredeemably cracked.

Mom always told the story of leaving San Francisco with a wistful look on her face. She said it was just her and her Mustang, crossing the Oregon border in 1980 and leaving behind a trail of lost friends and the worst decisions. She talked about how she moved to Medford, and wanted to be a paramedic for Mercy Flights, all at the ripe old age of twenty-one. Her favorite part was always the helicopters. She says she liked how she could see the entirety of the valley for just a moment before descending from the sky, like an angel made of IVs and defibrillators.

When I was a kid, I always thought it made sense mom was a paramedic. She was my mom, which automatically made her a hero, and I figured if she was a hero to me, she must be a hero to everyone else.

My parents moved us all to Portland in 2000 so Mom could get a job at MetroWest, the biggest paramedic company in the state. Mom worked for Metro as a paramedic and a trainer and helped in many areas. I was too young to remember anything back then, but from the way everyone around me talks about it, I know two things: Mom was good at her job, and she loved it more than anything.

It was my fault Mom stopped being a paramedic.

Working for Metro was brutal in a way Mercy Flights wasn't. Mom was used to picking up injured hikers out of the mountains. It was not the type of violence that comes with living in a suburb in the biggest city of the state. But Portland is a beast no one wants to acknowledge, and when you're the one in the ambulance, you don't have the option of turning around.

My sister told me it was a summer night deep in July of 2004. Just a few days before, Mom had called her and me into our upstairs bedroom so she could toss an unripe pumpkin out onto the patio below and show us exactly what would happen to us if we played near the open window during the incoming heatwave. I'm not sure if I remember this happening or if I've just been told about it so many times the memory has become super-imposed over another memory, but what I do know is we never played near the window again.

The ambulance had been idling in the Burger King parking lot down the road when they got a call about a hit and run, less than a mile from the side street my house lived on. It wasn't an unusual type of call in the bright suburbs, where everything revolves around the street level highways: Tualatin-Valley Highway, 185th and Canyon, merging in a clash of traffic and a lack of stop signs.

That night, it was a little girl. Her hair was the color of washed-out platinum, stained with dirt and blood from the tires. She was small for her age, as if she were born prematurely and never quite came back from it. Her nose was perfectly straight, no little button to press, and her face was scrunched like she was simply sleeping.

There were only two real differences between us.

My eyes, a bright hazel like an autumn chestnut. Hers, a sea-swept blue, the same shade as my mother's.

Me, alive and sprawled out in the hallway at the house as I waited for my mom to get home from work. Her, curled up on the road like her little limbs had any chance of protecting her.

I don't know how the story ends.

By all accounts, Mom came home at the end of her shift, picked me up off the floor of the hallway and put me to bed the same way she did every morning. She went to therapy for a few weeks after it, before resigning from her career of twenty-five years to become a Comcast saleswoman. We continued with our lives, and she raised me the same as she always had; we ended up alright.

Reality doesn't work that way.

I was four years old.

My sister says it went like this.

Mom came home at five a.m. and stepped over my sleeping form to grab the new Marlboro Golds Dad had bought off the kitchen table. She went out to the garage and smoked the entire pack as my dad woke up and got ready for work. For the first time in my life, I woke up on the floor of the hallway where I went to sleep instead of back in my bed.

Mom went to bed and slept for fifteen hours straight. Grandma cooked us breakfast, lunch and dinner and fed us and played with us all day. No one asked where mom was. We knew.

I could say mom was different after. It wouldn't be a lie; it just wouldn't be the truth.

I wasn't old enough to know what it was like before. I don't remember the incident. All I remember was what Mom told me sitting at the kitchen table, years after it happened, mixed in with the muddled memories of what my sister explained to me in the weeks after. Two completely different stories, both having the same ending.

The earliest memory of my mom that is truly my own is when I was five. My hair was down past my shoulders, a perfectly straight sheet of platinum, only able to be attained by being under the age of eight. I was a child who loved rolling on the ground, so my hair was always a rat's nest instead of the perfect wig it was capable of being. I didn't know how to take care of it because it just didn't matter to me.

I'm sure Mom brushed my hair every night, but I only ever remember it happening on Tuesdays. Maybe that was because it always felt like a Tuesday, or maybe it was just because we always seemed to be watching American Idol when she did it and I knew it only aired Tuesday nights. I remember the feeling of a large paddle brush ripping across my scalp and the way my mom would threaten to cut off my hair if I didn't learn how to keep it smooth.

By the time I reached elementary school, I had the habit of keeping a little hairbrush in my backpack. I would brush my hair during class, knowing it was disruptive and made my teachers angry, but when I got home at the end of the school day, Mom would run her fingers through my hair, and I knew she was proud of me.

I was a messy kid. I was dealing with undiagnosed ADHD and a budding hatred for authority. My favorite way to store my clothes was throwing them across my bedroom and just remembering where they landed.

I thought my system flawless. Mom thought it disrespectful.

I came home from school to find she had taken all my clothes off the floor and stuffed them into trash bags hidden in the back of the garage. She said I could get them back when I learned to respect them.

She never gave them back, instead she chose not to say anything when I stole them out of the garage a few weeks later.

They were back on my floor by the end of the day.

Rumors by Fleetwood Mac is Mom's favorite album. It was the soundtrack to nearly every part of my childhood, but the day I associated it with the most came when I was fourteen.

Mom's go-to way of bonding with me was taking me on little trips. It was a two-hour drive to the coast from Portland and while I hated the sea, it was Mom's favorite place, so I always said I'd go when she asked. That weekend, we had gotten permission to spend the night at a friend's apartment in Rockaway, as long as we fed the cats. It was fun to explore the little tourist traps along the boardwalk, and I came away from the beach with more sand in my hair than I wanted to admit.

We drove the long way home, on Highway 6. Mom let me pick the music for the first half of the drive and I picked *Rumors* because I knew it was what she would've picked herself. The smile she gave me when the opening bars of *Second Hand News* started playing was enough to make up for all the sand.

Highway 6 was special, because while it wasn't as old or famous as Highway 1, it had the same type of feeling. Highway 6 cut further east than 1, going directly over the tops of the coastal mountains dividing Oregon. Right at the top of the highway, there was a giant satellite dead spot. No calls came in or out from there, and the closest sign of civilization was the Government station fifteen miles down the mountain.

The car wreck was in the middle of the dead spot. It was a four-car pile-up, right along the cliff side. Our car was a mile behind when it happened, and when the traffic moved to let us pass the damage, Mom pulled the wheel of our SUV hard to the side and turned the engine off, right in the middle of *The Chain*. She looked me dead in the eyes and I wondered for just a moment if she ever regretted how my eyes were a different color than hers.

"I'm going to help them," she said, her voice even and smooth like the timbre of someone who is used to being in charge. "You can either get out and help me, or you can stay right here where I know where you are."

I was out the door before she could finish the sentence.

It was the first time I saw a dead body. Mom had climbed right into the man's car to check his pulse and when she found none, she called the time of death out into the air. It didn't mean anything to me, but I knew it should've.

We weren't the only people to stop and help, but Mom was the one with the most experience. She gathered her little crew of people and set them to work, checking damages and heading down the mountain to call for help. Mom waved at me to follow her and went over to one of the cars, flipped and propped against the mountainside.

The people inside were still alive. Mom told me to get the boxcutter out of the back of our car and when I returned, she used it to help the people out of their seatbelts and onto the ground.

It was a man and a woman, and my job was to hold the woman's hand and keep her calm as Mom tried to keep the man conscious and alive until the paramedics got there.

The woman was thirty years old and cried into my teenage arms for the entire half hour it took for rescue to get there.

The paramedics shooed Mom and I away when we got there. We would only be a hindrance from that point on, so we bundled back into our SUV and drove the rest of the way home.

Mom told me she was proud of me as the wreck disappeared in the rearview mirror. I'm sure she told me she was proud of me at some other point in time, but whenever I try to remember, all I can hear is her saying it as *Gold Dust Woman* played softly on the car radio.

We made it to the end of Highway 6 before my adrenaline rush wore off. When I fell asleep, I dreamt of being a paramedic.

I woke up as we parked in the driveway of our house with the distinct understanding if I ever became a paramedic, Mom would kill me.

I started realizing I wasn't a girl somewhere around sophomore year of high school. It's been so long I can't even fully remember it anymore. All I remember is the itchiness of it all. I have eczema, like my dad, and always blamed the itch on it. It is easy to ignore the way your skin crawls when you have a decade old prescription for steroid cream in the bathroom cabinet.

The first true sign was women's deodorant. Because of my eczema, I don't sweat much, and I always chalked my hatred of women's deodorant up to pure unfamiliarity. I was a smart teenager. I knew if I thought about it for too long, it would ruin my life or at least it seemed like it would.

Turns out trying not to think of something only makes you think about it more and I came out as non-binary to everyone except my family during my senior year. It was a soft launch of a coming out, all of it taking place in my Instagram bio. I blocked Mom right before I changed my name to a shortened version of what it had always been. The only people who called me by my new name were the ones who cared enough to notice.

A week after, I sent out my college applications. I applied to ten schools and got into exactly one. It wasn't my top choice, but it certainly felt like fate had decided I needed a heavy hand.

I moved to Ashland in the fall, and it wasn't lost on me that it was the same place Mom had run to forty years before.

I moved back in with my parents at the age of twenty for three months. There wasn't anywhere else for me to go during the summer of 2020, and while I knew there was a high likelihood it would kill me, living with my parents was better than trying to find somewhere else to go.

During August, Mom came upstairs and sat herself on my bed as I worked on a project at my desk. She was back at Metro again, this time as dispatcher. It was different and the same as before.

She seemed happier and it was the only credit I was willing to give.

Mom looked at me through the thick lens of her glasses. She had the same wrinkle in between her eyebrows I always got when I was trying to figure out how to say something complicated.

In the end, she asked just a simple question.

"Do you not respect me?"

My knee-jerk reaction was to tell her, "Yes." I respected her on some level but not like this. Not when she was using it against me.

In the end, the real issue was I had left the kitchen a mess the night before. She thought I had done it on purpose to spite her. I had known for years she thought I was out to get her. It was nice to finally get confirmation.

During that same summer, she taught me how to take a shot of Fireball. It burned as it went down my throat.

"It's all in the breathing, baby girl," she said to me. "It's all in the breathing."

I don't hold any hatred for my mom. I'm older than she was when she moved to Oregon. We have, at our core, grown up in entirely different realities but I always can and always will see the echoes of her in me. From the way I laugh when I'm putting up a front or the way watching Fleetwood Mac's Rumors turn on my record player makes me cry. I know Mom is a part of me. She always has been, and always will be.

Maybe growing up isn't so much of growing past our parents. Maybe it's just realizing they were once people like you.

My mom turned 62 this year. I sent her a text wishing her a happy birthday.

I turned 22 this year. She sent me a text wishing me happy birthday.

On my birthday I took a shot of Fireball next to my kitchen sink, while my friends laughed at the dining room table. It burned going down, but I breathed through my nose, just like Mom taught me.

It isn't perfect, but it works.

The Ashes

jr murray

No one was particularly shocked when Barbara died. Her tragic ending had seemed inevitable, if not imminent. She herself probably would've agreed. There was a brief article, just a paragraph or two, with an accompanying photograph in the local paper of what was left of her house, an unremarkable, one-story, white clapboard ranch she'd inherited from her parents. That's how my parents found out, even though the piece only described the unidentified remains of a single victim found at the address. I never saw the picture, never wanted to, since it would just add a visual component to the sadness. I know it was taken before sunrise, after the fire had been extinguished. I can't help but imagine a true-crime-style photograph with the camera flash highlighting the starkness of what was left of the house's frame: still-smoldering two-by-fours collapsed into indecipherable chaos. The contents of the house would be reduced to heaps of ash and debris, and the thick New England woods surrounding it would be mostly black, except for an occasional branch or cluster of leaves bleached out by the camera flash against a black backdrop.

My parents called my brother and told him. He and Barbara hadn't spoken in months; he was inconsolable then and months afterward, often bursting into tears at the thought of her or the mention of her name. On a visit to California eight months after she died, during a dinner party at my house, the subject of Barbara came up, and his crying started. My friend, Josh, an actor who's kind and empathic, led him to the back porch and consoled him for an hour and a half. Josh didn't know my brother often cried, without reservation and about a variety of things, but his sadness about Barbara was genuine. It still is. Although he no longer weeps when he talks about her, she remains integral to his identity, and over twenty years later, he often and fondly reminisces about her.

So do I, albeit in different ways. I was seven years old, and they were sixteen when Barbara entered the picture. Still, I absorbed (perhaps viscerally, if not intellectually) my brother's romantic appreciation of what was, for her and her family, the humiliating transition from Polish aristocracy to struggling refugees. Even now, her story of cruelty, toil, and doom seems like something from a gothic novel. She was unique to anyone else I knew; for all her struggles, she had a majestic, slightly aloof quality, suggesting she was a little better than everyone else. She'd already survived the sorts of challenges most middle-class American kids couldn't fathom. Most people I knew took for granted (or denied) the safety nets they had growing up in relatively stable families. They expected the world to respond to them in certain ways and it usually did. Barbara had no such support, so she had no such expectations. This might be what my brother found so alluring about her: she wasn't shackled to established notions about the way things should look, but how the way things should be.

They were star-crossed lovers who weren't really lovers, even though they'd been married and divorced. With the odd logic, which can be unconsciously applied when something doesn't make sense is so familiar, everyone considered them a couple, since they exhibited a physical comfort with each other, which seemed more romantic than platonic. After meeting in 1968 at a summer program for high school students at a local university, they became intertwined until her death. When they weren't speaking, he regularly talked about why they weren't speaking, the insinuation being they'd be talking again before too long.

They qualified as "star-crossed" for many reasons, including how both sets of parents disapproved of the union, how each of them wrestled with demons such as mental illness and addiction, and how they could swing between adoring and detesting each other, often over the course of one evening. But perhaps what doomed the union was my manly brother is also very—and unabashedly—gay, something Barbara learned soon after they were together. Certainly, a disappointment, but something she said she could live with. She even joked about it. When they were living together, he became obsessed with Marianne Faithful's 1979 album *Broken English*. When Faithful sang the line from the song "Why'd Ya Do It?"—*"Every time I see your dick, I see her cunt in our bed!"*—Barbara took a pull off her cigarette and said with a dead-eyed smirk, "Well, at least I'll never have to worry about *that*." She was accustomed to his late-night, hours-long "errands" to "The Bluefish Bowl," his pseudonym for a gay bar. Still, he claimed all she wanted was for him to "knock her up, give her a couple of kids," and she wouldn't make any other demands on him. Anyone would look at them and assume they were a couple, since they often behaved romantically: cuddling, kissing, speaking in low voices, getting jealous of friends of the opposite sex. When they fought, she would withdraw into silence, chain-smoking and staring blankly into space, wallowing in her sadness while he would rant, slam doors, and throw things. Everyone who spent any length of time with them had seen this ugly dynamic play out at some point. It was a volatile, passionate union, and they weren't ashamed to show it. My brother regularly proclaimed, "I want to clear the air—get it all out in the open. I don't go for that repression stuff." Unfortunately for people around him, including Barbara, his "clearing the air" in a state of fury required passivity from anyone who didn't want his anger to escalate, leaving him with the assumption their silence or exit was tacit acceptance of his righteousness.

Before age and substance abuse took their physical tolls, they made an alluring couple. He was six-foot-two with light-blue eyes, broad shoulders, high cheekbones, and a deep, velvety voice. She was average height and curvy, with thin but wavy blond hair, big, light-green eyes with Garbo-esque sunken lids, pore-less skin, and a trace of an indiscernible but clearly European accent. They both smoked relentlessly and looked good doing it. Each had friends of their own and little tolerance for someone who didn't stimulate their particular interests. Each was a voracious reader, and while my brother had exceptional artistic talent, which no doubt made him more enthralling to her, Barbara's talent was more academic, which he respected. In many ways they epitomized the counterculture, and from the perspective of someone a decade younger, it looked great, with all its uninhibition and unpredictability, never mind style.

Barbara's parents escaped Poland during the Second World War and temporarily settled in London, where she was born, until moving to the U.S. when she was eight. At times she sounded British, but her words ending with "ing" sounded like "ink," hinting at Eastern European influence. Her last name was Worelkiewicz, which she pronounced Vorel-KEH-vitch, even though locals pronounced it as the much less exotic "Worolkuhwits." My brother liked to tease her about it, claiming her pronunciation was nothing more than pretense. She was an only child, and although her college-educated parents worked in a laboratory at a large pharmaceutical company, they were raging alcoholics, blackout drunk every night but out the door heading to work at 7:30 every morning. Barbara spoke freely about their proclivities (drinking, smoking, crying, mourning, fighting, accusing, and more drinking) and mused about them teaching her the party trick of making cocktails for them and their friends by the time she was six years old. This was also the age she first experienced drunkenness, which she said made them laugh as she stumbled around the living room. Still, she took pride in claiming her parents were aristocrats who'd lost everything in the war and who were now doomed to earn a living and survive a middle-class existence surrounded by the philistines who dominated that small New England factory town.

For all her Slavic pessimism and resignation, Barbara had this magnetic energy, and I loved being with her. She'd discuss anything and if something struck her as funny, she'd toss her head back and laugh her hearty smoker's laugh. She was so different from any of the females in my family, who were attractive, intelligent, and opinionated feminists. They were more traditional in the way they were the products of stable parents and Catholic school. I admired Barbara's unintentional naughtiness, such as saying "fuck" in front of my very proper mother, catching herself, and then saying, "oh, shit!"—which elicited a good-natured raising of my mother's eyebrows, a stifled laugh from me, and a playful scolding from my brother. He attributed such behavior to the twisted or lacking parenting skills of serious alcoholics more consumed with their own needs than with their only child's. On a weekend home from college, they might dote on her and buy her extravagant gifts for no reason, but a half of a bottle of vodka later, her mother would remind her she was the result of not one, but two failed abortion attempts, and how they never wanted a child.

One drunken Christmas Barbara presented her mother with a few tchotchkes hurriedly purchased during a couple of brief breaks from her work. After opening each gift her mother's weeping intensified, exclaiming the same thing in her thick, Polish accent, "Oh, my Got, eez so beautiful! You give me everythingk and I give you nothingk!"

Her mother then sent her to rummage through the cluttered dining room table to retrieve her own Christmas gift: a brand new but unboxed and unwrapped platinum and diamond bracelet still bearing its hefty price tag. It looked like it had been tossed where it landed: next to a dirty coffee cup on top of a stack of old newspapers. Barbara went to bed that night pleased with her mother's reaction to her modest gifts, but when she was about to drive off early the next morning, her mother called out from the front door, "Hanya!" (her pet name for Barbara). "Vait a minute!" Barbara sat in her idling car for a minute before her mother walked down the driveway in her housecoat and slippers, carrying a brown paper grocery bag. She went to the passenger-side door, opened it, and chucked the bag on the seat. "Take dis back. I don't need any of dis shit." Inside were all the tchotchkes she'd been so enamored with the night before.

Having grown up with depressed, addicted parents, Barbara was used to this sort of bait-and-switch game, and as an only child with no friends, she had few buffers for their cruelty, few ways to gain perspective. Mercilessly teased by other children for her thick Polish accent as a young schoolgirl in London, her mother supposedly took pity on her one afternoon and presented her with a new dress. When Barbara strutted onto the schoolyard the next morning confident everything was about to change, she became the immediate laughing-stock of the school. As a practical joke, her mother had her put the dress on backwards, insisting it was the latest style. Even as an old woman, her mother still thought the gag was a winner.

Despite an upbringing which might've sealed her doom early on, there was an optimism, a determination, in Barbara when she was young. She was confident of her intelligence and, with little effort, excelled academically, breezing through her undergraduate degree and a master's in English while working full time. Her reading habits were eclectic: dense classics, feminist theory, trashy romance, poetry, and magazines. She relished a good story—reading one, telling one, or hearing one—and she was precise about language. I'd tease her about using the exact same phrasing when repeating a story, such as describing a camping trip with friends who'd arranged the picnic tables "in a horseshoe affair" outside her tent in anticipation of her making everyone breakfast. But she also appreciated a good, bawdy joke. Once I hit adolescence, it brought us even closer, since she was a rich source for and happy recipient of new material. She hadn't been indoctrinated into American middle-class propriety, so if a story was well structured and well told, and a good joke demands precise structure and language, she appreciated it. If it wasn't good, she didn't appreciate it.

With her quick wit, sharp tongue, and droll delivery, she often caught people off guard with her straight-faced but hilarious comebacks. In her late twenties she worked at a government agency in Hartford writing grants. She had a chauvinistic boss named Dick, who proudly promoted only the men and hit on all the young women, even though he was newly married. He was a font of loudmouthed, sexist proclamations who ruined what could've been a tolerable job for her. A committed feminist, she couldn't abide him and made no qualms about it, so they were a constant source of irritation to each other. The day after his son was born, he walked into the middle of the office and proudly proclaimed the baby had the biggest penis he'd ever seen. Before anyone could conjure up some sort of response, Barbara offered a deadpan retort of, "On an adult or on a baby?" Everyone in the office, except for Barbara and her stunned boss, burst out laughing. I was seventeen when she told me this story, and it made me laugh hard, but it also made me respect her daring choices which seem to reflect someone who derived strength from having nothing to lose.

While grant writing, Barbara kept a room at the YMCA in Hartford, which had the atmosphere of a college dormitory, albeit with a much more ethnically and socioeconomically diverse population of women than most college dormitories had then or have now. She had her banged-up, bright-green AMC Gremlin, and would drive to see her parents for a weekend or to meet my brother at some halfway point, where they'd get into some mischief, sometimes with hilarious results. One weekend when her parents were away, they decided to go to the house to drop acid, which prompted a midnight drive through the countryside of eastern Connecticut. Inspired by a beautiful, moonlit pasture, they parked the car, hopped the fence, and found a cozy spot on the grass where they could sit and polish off a bottle of wine. When the boulder next to them began to move, they attributed it to the acid until it stood up, revealing itself to be a groggy bull.

After her weekends of debauchery, she returned to her rented room in Hartford.

One woman living at the Y who'd befriended her, came into her room one day to say she could see Barbara's potential, but she was concerned by some of the poor choices she was making. The woman presented her with a paperback copy of Joan Crawford's *My Way of Life*, a guidebook for achieving female fulfillment. Barbara and my brother howled with laughter as they read it, studying its many photographs. There were photos of Crawford posing in her Fifth Avenue penthouse, supervising her elderly maid, whom she referred to as "Mamacita," meticulously stuffing the sleeves of her dresses with tissue paper, or attending some social gathering—including her daughter's wedding—where every eye in the room was on her instead of the bride. Touting her expertise as a hostess, she recommends—when having a "dear friend" over for dinner (in her case, Anita Loos)—it's best to set up a card table in the living room and serve something informal, such as pork chops. The book was a model of 1960s camp. What was particularly comical to Barbara was her acquaintance at the Y thought this specific book would provide an avowed feminist who drank, smoked, cussed, went to graduate school while she worked full time, and lived at the YMCA a path she'd been seeking. But no clear path to fulfillment, personal or professional, would exist for Barbara.

Perhaps there was partial fulfillment in the periods when she and my brother set up housekeeping in one apartment or another. He always dictated the décor with his collection of "oddball" antiques, including prosthetic limb and glass eye collections, and heavy curtains to keep it dark during the day. His music choices complemented the ambiance: Velvet Underground, Brian Eno, Rolling Stones—played loud enough to make casual conversation effortful. She paid all the bills. Their attempts at domesticity never lasted a full year, since he would end the situation with his predictable lament of how he felt smothered and he "never wanted to have an old lady."

It was during one of those attempts at domesticity they decided, probably after a few cocktails, they should be married, something Barbara had been advocating for years. On a sunny Wednesday afternoon, she put into action her long-established plan, including the justice of the peace, an 82-year-old woman who lived in an antique-filled Victorian house on a country road. When they arrived, the woman situated the two of them in her living room to chat for a while before performing the ceremony. She'd evidently gotten a favorable enough impression of them to ask if she could invite her two friends in the other room, who'd come over for a cup of tea, to watch the ceremony. Barbara and my brother, charmed by the idea of who they'd imagined would be two more old women in the mold of the J.P., were surprised when she returned from the kitchen with her friends in tow, two middle-aged women wearing matching tank tops and donning crew cuts and tattoos. "Meet my friends," the J.P. said, "Friday and Leavenworth." Barbara and my brother were delighted by the addition to the ceremony.

If Barbara hoped marriage would guarantee the realization of her romantic ambitions, she was soon disenchanted. My brother was feeling trapped a few months later and made his predictable exit. It was the end of their attempts to cohabitate.

Barbara mostly lived alone as she went through a series of grant-writing jobs until she landed a job teaching at a small secretarial "college," which didn't pay much but allowed her to live for free at her mother's house. Her mother was receptive to the situation, as she'd gotten lonely following her retirement from work and the death of Barbara's father. Although her mother, Lydia, could still be cruel when she was drunk, she'd mellowed over the years, and the two of them became obsessive gardeners, mycologists, and pet rescuers. Gone were the elegant Borzoi dogs and Siamese cats of Barbara's youth, replaced by rescue cats who peed in the house and a fat, flatulent basset hound mix they named "Yeltsin." After some rigorous gardening on hot summer days, Lydia and Barbara would drag out the "Mr. Turtle" plastic kiddie pool they'd bought. Taking advantage of the foliage shielding them from neighbors, they'd lie in Mr. Turtle naked, reading books, smoking cigarettes, and drinking cocktails, grateful for some relief from the heat and humidity of a Connecticut summer.

As the years passed, Barbara's alcoholism progressed, and she transitioned from leaving jobs of her own volition to being fired. I was in my thirties by then. On a visit to the East Coast to see my parents, Barbara stopped by on her way to teach a class one afternoon. I hadn't seen her for at least five years, and it seemed her pessimism and her sense of doom, that had always been chasing her, had finally caught up and drowned out any optimism. It was consuming her. Now suffering from full-blown diabetes, she'd gained about thirty pounds and wore thick glasses with a brownish tint, dimming her bright-green eyes and leaving the impression she had dark circles under them. Her hair was brown, short, and thin, and when she turned her head at certain angles, you could see the curve of her scalp. Her black sweater was sprinkled with cigarette ashes and animal hair, and she smelled like a combination of the More cigarettes she smoked and last night's vodka. Perhaps what was most unsettling was her sense of humor. Even in the form of sarcasm, it was undetectable. In retrospect, it's no surprise the tenor of her student evaluations from the secretarial school declined from tepid to livid, eventually leading to the cessation of her contract.

Always a hard worker and determined to make her own money, a series of jobs followed. After scoring well on the postal exam, she started delivering mail on a rural route near her mother's house. Driving one of those little mail trucks with the right-side driver's seat presented a challenge since she'd always been a terrible driver in a regular car. She had to use her gardening skills to repair several flower beds on her own after working all day, and she had to pay out of pocket to have a professional gardener repair the wheel marks she carved into one irate customer's lawn. Mounting complaints about her driving, including ruined landscapes and downed mailboxes, combined with multiple reports of the wrong mail in the wrong box, led to a series of warnings, followed by her eventual firing.

No longer forced to earn a living since her diabetes had become debilitating, she often fell asleep after following her nightly routine of reading in bed, smoking cigarettes, and sipping from her giant glass of vodka on the nightstand. My brother knew about this dangerous habit, since he still visited her occasionally, and warned her of a disastrous ending when he saw the cigarette burns on her pillowcase and sheets. No devotee to cleanliness himself, he was appalled by the condition of her house, and he'd tease her by saying: "It looks like the people moved out and the bums moved in, then the bums moved out and the bears moved in, then the bears moved out and you moved in." I expect she mustered up a chuckle from this.

Convinced she was on a collision course to disaster, my brother insisted he wanted a divorce. They hadn't lived together in years, and neither of them had some romantic prospect pushing for them to disentangle. My brother, however, was convinced Barbara would, as she often did, get behind the wheel of her car blind drunk and cause a serious accident, leaving him vulnerable to a lawsuit. His apprehension baffled me, considering his meager, arguably nonexistent assets. Yes, his antiques no doubt had some value—more as cultural artifacts than serious commodities—but he drove my mother's old car, my parents paid his insurance and part of his rent, and he worked in a candy and cigarette shop at one of the local casinos. I doubt any litigious accident victim would think they hit the jackpot once they delved into his situation. With her mother now dead, Barbara was the one with all the assets. She didn't care about them, so long as she had enough to stay in her house and fill her basic needs. Still, he got his divorce, an amicable one. Living her life in a daily blur had rendered Barbara apathetic about the whole thing.

Despite what a difficult union it was, they were profoundly connected to each other, unable to be fully unified but unable to detach. The last few times my brother saw her, he would be devastated by her drunken resignation to her life of misery, tearfully recounting how he pleaded with her: "Choose life, Hanya, choose life!" It's important I don't paint him as some evil character, even though his behavior could be beastly. He did deeply love her, and he was cursed by it in the same way she was cursed by her love for him. It was the time, the circumstances, the mental illness, and the addiction.

Joan Didion said, "I don't know what I think until I write it down." It's possible in providing this extremely condensed recollection, with so many tragic, hysterical, and even romantic details omitted, I'm trying to understand their story without the cultural filters, which relegate it to the bizarre, the absurd, and the pathetic. She's immortalized in the condo his siblings bought him after he squandered his inheritances, first from Barbara, then from my parents. The place smells like a neglected cat box, and it's cluttered with all his beloved oddball antiques. But there are small shrines to Barbara peppered throughout: school photos from London, a passport photo of her as a teenager, and perhaps most prophetic, a 35-millimeter black-and-white photo of her taken by my brother in their twenties. She's gazing to the side of the camera into the ether, clearly consumed with thought, the ever-present cigarette just a few short inches from her mouth, perched between the tips of her index and middle fingers of her suspended hand. It's a portrait of a mind occupied with too much experience, too much knowledge, too much feeling. If I shift to a different cultural lens, Barbara's life might not seem so tragic. She was—is loved by who she claimed was the one man she ever wanted. Maybe it wasn't a successful romance in the traditional sense, but it was what she got, and she felt it, embraced it, welcomed it in only the way a character from a gothic novel could. This embrace seemed congruent with the rest of her life; chronic disappointment in a loved one's behavior might've been a comfortable old shoe for her. Maybe she embraced her disillusionment and her demise, like Daphne du Maurier's character of Mrs. Danvers going down in the flames of Manderley to be at one with her beloved former mistress of the house, Rebecca.

At this point my brother looks a decade older than he is, thanks to years of substance abuse, cigarette smoking, and, in recent years, relentless back pain. No longer a drinker but a chronic pot smoker, he's now nicer to me—to everyone—than he's ever been, possibly because with Barbara and my parents gone, he tacitly depends on his siblings to hold up his safety nets—and we do. His temper has finally calmed: no more yelling, no more mood swings, no more paranoia, and just a trace of the narcissism which was once a dominant character trait. Comfortably surrounded by his antiques and his movie collection, he has an iPhone, but is determined to remain computer illiterate. If the spirit moves him, he does some artwork. He has few complaints with his life, which he considers having been a full one. There's no remorse for how he treated Barbara, but there's also no regret about the years he invested in their relationship. He's convinced of his own righteousness in how he navigated a union with some very complicated dynamics. I don't think Barbara would be particularly surprised.

Issue 13 Contributors

Nicholas Barnes earned a Bachelor of Arts in English from Southern Oregon University in 2019. He is currently working as an editor in Portland. His poems have appeared in over fifty publications including *trampset*, *NonBinary Review*, and *Eclectica Magazine*. His least favorite season is summer. His favorite soda is RC Cola.

Roger Camp lives in Seal Beach, CA where he muses over his orchids, walks the pier, plays blues piano and spends afternoons reading under an Angel's Trumpet with a charm of hummingbirds. When he's not at home, he's photographing in the Old World. His work has appeared in *Pank*, *Rust+Moth*, *Gulf Coast*, *Southern Poetry Review*, *Nimrod* and is forthcoming in *The Scientific American*.

Katherine Van Eddy is a California-born poet who now lives in Washington State. Her poems have appeared in journals such as *Common Ground Review*, *Creative Colloquy*, *Gold Man Review*, *Cirque*, and *Clover*. She has a BA in Creative Writing, MAT in Elementary Education, and MFA in Poetry from Pacific Lutheran University. Katherine loves mothering her two kids and cat, Dexter, and she feels most at home anywhere near water.

Linda Ferguson is an award-winning writer of poetry, fiction and essays. Her chapbook *Of the Forest* was the 2nd place winner of The Poetry Box Chapbook Prize 2021, and her most recent collection, *Not Me: Poems About Other Women*, was published by Finishing Line Press. As a writing teacher, she has a passion for helping students find their voice and explore new territory. https://bylindaferguson.blogspot.com/

Elizabeth Galoozis's poems have appeared in *Air/Light, Pidgeonholes, RHINO, Witness, Sinister Wisdom,* and elsewhere. She serves as a reader for *The Maine Review* and *Abandon Journal.* Elizabeth was selected by Claire Wahmanholm for AWP's Writer to Writer Program in 2022. She works as a librarian and lives in southern California. Elizabeth can be found on Twitter and Instagram at @thisamericanliz, and at her website https://elizabethgaloozis.wordpress.com/.

Melody Greenfield, a Los Angeles native, earned her MFA in 2015 from Antioch University LA, where she studied CNF (creative nonfiction). Since then, she's been published widely in literary journals, including in *Brevity, The Los Angeles Review,* the *Los Angeles Review of Books, The Manifest-Station, Hippocampus Magazine,* and elsewhere. Greenfield was nominated for a Best of the Net award by *Kelp Journal* and has a flash essay forthcoming in *Awakenings: Stories of Body & Consciousness* anthology.

Tim Haywood is a graphic designer and writer in Seattle. When not spending time with his wife and daughters, he enjoys nurturing his blog, "Reflections of a Shallow Pond," the curmudgeonly ramblings of a tail-end Boomer. His short stories have appeared in publications and magazines including *Gulf Stream Literary Magazine, Twisted Vine Literary Arts Journal, Potato Soup Literary Journal,* and *Schuylkill Valley Journal.*

Heikki Huotari attended a one-room school and spent summers on a forest-fire lookout tower. Since retiring from academia/mathematics he has published poems in numerous journals and in five poetry collections. His manuscript, To Justify The Butterfly, won second prize, and publication, in the 2022 James Tate Chapbook Competition. His Erdős number is two.

Chris Menezes has his BA in creative writing from CSU Long Beach and MFA in poetry from Converse College. His work has appeared in many literary journals throughout the years and he's currently working on getting his first book published. He lives in Southern California with his wife and dog, where he makes money as a copywriter and tries to surf and play music as much as possible. Find him online at christophermenezes.com

Eric P. Mueller lives in Northern California with his partner and two dogs. He enjoys red wine and soft pretzels. His essays and book reviews have appeared in *Talking River*, *Vagabond City Review*, *Boudin*, *Foglifter*, *The Ignatian*, and elsewhere.

JR Murray was a professor of writing at USC for two decades where he emphasized collaborations between his students and partners from the surrounding community. He splits his time between Los Angeles and the Mendocino Coast and often wonders what he was thinking when he adopted the third dog. His recent work has appeared or is forthcoming in *The Los Angeles Times*, *Avalon Literary Review*, *Big Muddy*, *Delmarva Review*, *El Portal*, *Opiate*, and *The MacGuffin*.

Nicole Pyles is a writer living in Portland, Oregon. When she's not hunting down the right word, she's talking to God, reviewing books on her writing blog, watching movies, hanging out with family, and daydreaming. Her work has been featured in *Ripley's Believe it or Not*, *WOW! Women on Writing*, *The Voices Project*, *Sky Island Journal*, and *Arlington Literary Journal*. Her poetry was also featured in the anthology *Dear Leader Tales*. Read her musings at WorldofMyImagination.com.

Oliver Reimers is a writer from Sacramento, California. His work has been featured in *Prime Number Magazine* and *One Teen Story*. His one-act play "Something to Talk About" won a gold prize at the 2023 Lenaea Theater Festival. When he's not writing, Oliver enjoys playing piano, drawing, and reading. His favorite book is *A Separate Peace* by John Knowles.

Andrew Robin lives and writes with gratitude on Lopez Island (Sx'wálech) in the unceded ancestral waterways of the Coast Salish peoples. His latest is a chapbook called *Small Pale Telegrams from the World* from Sixth Finch Books.

Cindy Veach is the author of *Her Kind* (CavanKerry Press) a 2022 Eric Hoffer Montaigne Medal finalist and Gloved Against Blood (CavanKerry Press) a finalist for the Paterson Poetry Prize and Massachusetts Center for the Book Must Read. Her poems have appeared in the *Academy of American Poets Poem-a-Day, AGNI, Michigan Quarterly Review, Poet Lore* and elsewhere. A recipient of the Philip Booth Poetry Prize and Samuel Allen Washington Prize, she is the poetry co-editor of *MER.*

Juliet Waller is a playwright, short story author, and playwriting & theater teacher. Her work has appeared in, *The Kenyon Review* (as a co-author), *The Lit Star Review,* Seattle's *Poetry on Buses,* and *3Elements Literary Review.* Her plays have been produced by a variety of Seattle theaters. Her short stories and plays often focus on disasters, large and small.

Isabelle Walker teaches poetry with California Poets in the Schools (CPITS) and the Juvenile Court and Community Schools of Santa Barbara County. Her work has appeared in *The Maine Review, December, The Santa Barbara Literary Journal, Seven Hills Review,* the anthology *While You Wait,* among other journals. She has an MFA in Creative Nonfiction and Poetry from Antioch University Los Angeles.

Beck M. Weiser is an emerging author from Portland, OR. They grew up right outside of the city and now spend most of their days knitting, working with elementary schoolers and day dreaming about Batman. Their favorite flavor of Yerba Mate is Lemon Elation.

www.ingramcontent.com/pod-product-compliance
Lightning Source LLC
Chambersburg PA
CBHW021929170626
46807CB00007B/3038